Will Cook for Rock & Roll

Will Cook for Rock & Roll

ELIZABETH HEATON

Library of Congress Control Number:		2014922843
ISBN:	Hardcover	978-1-5035-3066-9
	Softcover	978-1-5035-3067-6
	eBook	978-1-5035-3068-3

This is a work of fiction. Names, characters, places and incidents either are the product of the author's imagination or are used fictitiously, and any resemblance to any actual persons, living or dead, events, or locales is entirely coincidental.

This book was printed in the United States of America.

Rev. date: 01/05/2015

To order additional copies of this book, contact:
Xlibris
1-888-795-4274
www.Xlibris.com
Orders@Xlibris.com
701123

CONTENTS

Foreword by Graham Canterbury 11
Acknowledgments 13
Introduction 15

Chapter One 19

1. Chili Rellenos 20
2. Chicken Tamales 20
3. Truffled Eggs 22

Chapter Two 23

4. Fiery Eggplant Bruschetta 25
5. Liver Pat-Tay Mermaid's Tail 26

Chapter Three 27

6. Screaming Yellow Zonkers ala Liz 27
7. Simple Raspberry Jam Turnovers with Hot Chocolate Sauce 28
8. Dutch Lunch or Steak Tartarc 32
9. Keith's Shepherd Pie 33

Chapter Four 59

10. Red Caribbean Grouper with Potatoes and Peppers 68
11. Corn Bread 70
12. Conch Chowder with Shrimp 76
13. Bloody Crab—Vodka Cocktail 77
14. Lobster Sherry 81

15. Pasta Foo Foo Fazoo 84
16. Slammin' Salmon 85
17. Naked Al Fresco Fruit Salad 86
18. Colin's Hamburgers 90

Chapter Five 92

19. Poor Man's Pork Chops 95

A Cook 100
The Recipes 101

People's names have been changed
in this tale for their privacy.

To

My husband

My two brothers, Dennis and Floyd

My two sisters, Carol and Katherine

My nieces and nephews

My friend Gayle

FOREWORD
BY GRAHAM CANTERBURY

These two books, *From London to Laurel Canyon* and *Will Cook for Rock and Roll*, take the reader to a place *all* baby boomers were aware of and fantasized about but never dared to dream they could *ever* be a part of. These two crazy girls *actually* lived it, and at the time when they were so young, they thought it was how life was always going to be! We are fortunate their memories were intact enough to record it all for us to read, from shared memories and from well-kept diaries and journals.

You will never look at cooking in quite the same way!

ACKNOWLEDGMENTS

Thank you to

My publishing consultant,
Jimmy Barnett.

And to Lorraine for her help
in remembering all the stories!

And to all the craziest people I have known
in the music and cooking worlds.

Elizabeth Heaton is married to Colin, a guitarist in an English band formed in the sixties, and he is still working with three of the original members. They have three grown kids—two boys, who are musicians, and a daughter, who is a chef in the Bronx, New York City.

INTRODUCTION

Lorraine yelled into the phone, "Get your ass to LAX in the next two hours! I will be live—parked in the limo in front of TWA. Oh, and don't forget your fucking *poke*! You'll be cooking for the *band* after the concert!"

When I got one of those calls, I knew better than to piss her off, so I did what I always did. I grabbed my poke and stuffed it with two slightly underripe eggplants and my cooking stuff and didn't bother to worry about clothes; I just stuffed the bag to the top with extra changes of underwear. Back in the day (the '60s), there were *no worries* at the airports, *no* hassles, *no* drug-sniffing dogs, *no* diseases, *no* metal detectors, *no* puffers, *no* invasive body searches. *Hell*, you could even *smoke* on the plane!

I grabbed my fringed leather jacket since I knew it would be cold in England, and I figured I could pilfer clothes from Lorraine since we were about the same size—six feet tall and size 10 long.

At the time, I wore jeans that were twenty-eight inches at the waist and thirty-four inches in length. String beans were very much in fashion; the dexies we would take, keeping the appetite away, but it never hindered our capacity for our favorite libation of choice—champagne! She had a very fast metabolism and could shimmy down to a size 8 anytime she wanted by just not eating for two days! I was envious of that together we were a formidable team.

Back to check-in. The most you were required to do was let someone rifle through your bags.

I only had my poke, which I was carrying on the plane, and once the guy started digging down into my underwear, he got all red in the face and gave up the ghost! I'm sure they would not have allowed me to take eggplants from one country to another, but my philosophy was, if you don't get caught, go for it!

This is my story of how I shared a terrible childhood with my friend Lorraine and how, at seventeen, I was thrown out of my home by my father who had too many kids to take care of. I was the oldest of seven and was a borderline A student who had never been in trouble well, never caught for doing anything worthy of being thrown out. I did a lot of sneaking out my window and hitchhiking to Laurel Canyon every chance I got. It was the "center of the world" to me, and it was only an hour away from Long Beach, California. I was a *terrific* cook, learning every trick from my mom, who was a master. She could literally perform miracles on fifty dollars a week (which fed *nine* people for seven days back then!). But she had to buy the cheap cuts of meat, giant bags of beans and rice, produce with spots on it—basically the cheapest of everything—but man, could that woman cook! Her pork chops were *everyone*'s favorite, with layers of potatoes, onions, and sauerkraut with a dash of Worcestershire. Poor woman had to buy the *thinnest* pork chops you ever saw, hence all the other ingredients to fill you up! Lots of nights we had "something" in a cream sauce over toast—chipped beef in cream sauce on toast, tuna and peas in cream sauce on toast, mystery meat in cream sauce on toast! I admired her for doing the very best she could. She was very lenient with me, because my father was a despot who ruled with an iron fist (literally). She had gotten pregnant at nineteen and was 100 percent dominated by my dad. He would put a stick shift car in the driveway behind her station wagon so she could only go to the store when he told her to. I offered hundreds of times to teach her to drive stick, but she was too afraid. She lived out her fantasies through me. She secretly helped me once get ready for a motorcycle trip across the United States and Canada when I was seventeen (but that is another book!).

I went to Laurel Canyon, like all the other long-haired young girls, to seek my fortune, and fortune I found by making myself indispensable to whoever needed my services of cooking, cleaning, pet-sitting, house-sitting, sewing, embroidery, jean-mending, etc.

I met Lorraine, and things just took off. She was a stunning model, and she relied on her looks and her sparkling conversational wit, high intelligence, and wicked sense of humor to get her wherever she wanted to go, and everyone wanted and desired her presence. She was a classic diva. The old cliché of "she couldn't boil water" *actually applied to her.* She was a slob; when she stayed in one place for more than a few months (which was very rare), she would accumulate cats and kittens like mad. Eventually someone would have to take over and round them up (it was usually me). She was inexcusably tardy, talked incessantly on the phone, took *forever* to get ready for functions, would get drunk or high at the most inopportune moments, constantly *lose* things that were important (like *keys*, bills, and paperwork), buy stuff she would never use, and *everything* was a "desperate emergency disaster" almost daily that someone would have to solve for her. I don't think she ever cleaned a place in her life. *But I loved her to death!* She had miraculous and wonderful qualities too—generous, big-hearted, sympathetic, could laugh at herself, down to earth, bawdy, the *most* honest person I ever knew, she never did BS anyone (no matter who they were), and hilariously funny. She looked at the world in a kind of "cockeyed" way; that was simpatico with me. We had a deal that she would finance my way. I was always to accompany her to rock-and-roll "functions" before concerts, after concerts, backstage and in hotel rooms to provide provocative food and drink and create a mood of conviviality to the affair. She was the "centerpiece," and I was the "chef to the rockers." As long as I kept my place and showed up right on time to wherever she told me to be, we got along famously, and I never had to pay for anything. There were a few times she would be miffed when she knew I had received a tip, but it happened from time to time. It might be actual money or jewelry or perfume, etc. I would sell the jewelry, as I was too young at the time to realize the importance of diamonds, platinum, and gem stones to one's future security.

Lorraine was way ahead of me in those terms! I preferred the silver and turquoise of the day, which I thought complimented my Rita Coolidge style of denim from head to toe.

We had a good gig, and we knew it. So, so many parties. It was an era of the party. Rules of any kind were discarded like tissues. If the money was there, *anything* was possible.

CHAPTER ONE

I was in the midst of wrapping some freshly baked banana nut breads I had baked and cooled for a friend in a band who was out of town. He lived on the opposite side of Ridgedale Trail in Laurel, from where Jim Morrison lived, by the country store. I got a phone call from Lorraine that she had put together a "happening." She was in town, and there was to be a reception at one of the clubs on Sunset, for a "new" band with this cute, young guy who was a piano player and had joined one of the established bands who played the club scene weekly. He convinced the band to release a couple of guys and hire another guy besides himself, which dramatically changed their sound. It was rumored that he was from old money, and he dressed rather effeminately, with flamboyant embroidered suits and the ever-present scarves. Lorraine wanted him.

The house was packed. I asked what the theme might be (her mind was on him!), and she said, "I don't know! Think of something." I decided on Mexican. She dropped by and gave me the money. I went shopping! I learned at a young age how to make chili rellenos, and my mom and I always made tamales around Christmas time, since I could remember. It was a cheap way for my mom to give gifts to the relatives and neighbors.

I purchased tequila, limes, and margarita salt for glasses, large pasilla chilis, corn masa, corn husks, bottled dark beer, chicken, diced chilis in the can, cheese, flour, cream, etc. I went back to the house to assemble everything. Here are my recipes for chili rellenos and chicken tamales:

Chili Rellenos

Make a thin, light batter with flour, cream, salt, a pinch of sugar, and some club soda. Don't make it too thin, or it won't adhere to the chili. Take your pasillas, and slice them open down one side.

Reach in and pull out the seedpod. Do *not* remove the stem. Pack the chili with some shredded cooked chicken and a long chunk of cheese. Secure the opening with a toothpick. Prepare some oil. Dip the chili in the batter, and fry till golden brown. Set them on paper towels to cool.

Prepare your sauce. In a saucepan, blanch some chopped celery. When it's softened, discard the water and add two cans of tomato soup and some cream and a good teaspoon of red chili powder. Whip this together. Assemble your fried chilis in a large casserole dish, pour on the sauce, and top with grated cheese.

Bake at 350 until browned on top. Serve with warm flour tortillas.

Chicken Tamales

In a large bowl, mix 3 cups of corn masa with 2 bottles of dark beer, and add water to make a thick paste you can mold with your hands. Heat this mixture until hot. Take a dry corn husk in one hand, and spoon a handful of the masa into the center of the husk. Make a cavity. Add some shredded chicken and diced green chilis. Mold the masa to cover the insides. Tuck the bottom and top of the dry corn husk over the insides, and stack them in a rack on top of a large pan with boiling water. Pack them in so they don't unwrap. Steam for about 30 to 40 minutes. Take out the rack, and let them cool. Serve with sour cream and green chili verde sauce in the jar.

I hustled the food over to the club. I covered two six-foot tables with bright-colored serapes and filled a large Mexican hat with corn chips. I assembled pitchers of margaritas and glasses, all frosted with salt, with a big bucket of ice. At the last minute, I made a huge bowl of guacamole and squeezed lime juice over the top to keep it from turning black.

What can I say? There wasn't a single chip left! Everyone was bowled over. I added another feather to my cap, and a positive outcome to my growing rep, and Lorraine got to meet with her new beau. All was good in the kingdom and the kitchen.

I think at this point, I need to talk about my poke. Back in the day, a lot of females carried very large, fur-covered totes with big leather shoulder straps. When I say big, I mean *big*. I always had to carry mine on my back, over my shoulder. You could easily use these things as a weekend-getaway bag. But I was famous for what I always carried in mine.

Here is what I would stock in my poke. When I knew I was going to be in a remote area and be hard-pressed for certain things, when I knew I was going to be cooking for the music crowd.

Necessities for the Poke

garlic bulbs	sugar cubes	dried, toasted coconut
salt	white truffle oil	dried anchovies
pepper	baking soda	walnuts and cashews
saffron threads	dried cilantro leaves	onion powder
chili pepper flakes	annatto for rice	Tabasco
bouillon cubes	dried bell pepper flakes	curry powder
Tahitian vanilla beans	meyer limes	dry mustard
turmeric	smoked paprika	Chinese five spice
coriander	fennel seeds	Old Bay Seasoning
star anise pods	dried oregano	bay leaves
Ziploc baggy instant coffee	cardamom seeds	tricolor peppercorns
Chinese mustard	tamarind pods	dried dill weed
dried basil, rosemary, thyme	soy sauce	cinnamon sticks
dried sage	tin of tomato paste	cocoa powder
dried wild mushrooms	cinnamon	tincture bottle of oil

small jar of caviar	nutmegs	tincture bottle of rosewater
tea	small bottle of kitchen bouquet	70% cacao chocolate
chili powder	small bottle of liquid smoke	cumin

Sometimes, I had more; sometimes, I had less, but these were the "core" ingredients for whatever situation came along.

A lot of the huge country homes in the United Kingdom that the nouveau-riche music people acquired after success with their bands usually had outbuildings where the staff would tend to chickens, horses, gorgeous gardens, kitchen gardens, etc. It was usually not hard to get a basket of fresh eggs. These were *not* like the eggs I was used to from the Southern California supermarkets! These eggs were super fresh and *big*, and the yolks were huge and deeply colored.

Here is a winner I used to make around one to two, the afternoon after a huge party. This one just knocked everyone out. Simple but fantastically elegant.

Spectacular Truffled Eggs, Fit for a King or Queen of Rock!

Take 2 thick slices off a loaf of local peasant bread.

Toast and butter it.

Fry 4 fresh eggs, over easy.

Do not break the yolks; slide 2 eggs onto each slice of bread.

Take a cleaned truffle (white or black, Italian or French), and *thinly* slice with a vegetable peeler.

Place 4 or 5 slices on top of the eggs.

Drizzle with extravirgin olive oil.

Add a touch of salt and pepper.

Divine! Serve with (what else?) chilled Dom Pérignon.

This was Lorraine's fave and most requested recipe of mine. She liked caviar on the side. Who wouldn't?

CHAPTER TWO

"Lizzy! Wake up and answer the damn phone!"

Lizzy is what Lorraine called me—my full nickname was Lizzy Borden, you know, the chick with the axe who gave her father forty whacks, and all that yuck-yuck, I didn't mind it though. I kind of liked her calling me Lizzy, and I had a nickname for her too. I called her LaLa.

The LaLa and Lizzy Show.

So she told me we were going to Heathrow, where we will be met by her "amour's" limo and straight away to the house in the countryside. Remember those two eggplants I told you about? This was the trip where they accompanied me. I knew at the time that the British *loved* their hot and spicy Indian food, their curry, and let's not forget their fish and chips! I planned on making an appetizer for everyone when the drinks were flowing and after the doobies were done. I made my fiery eggplant bruschetta with homemade Indian nan bread (kind of like pita that you tear apart).

The party was a veritable who's who of current rock and rollers and their ladies in waiting. It was a *very* male-dominated time, even though it was supposedly the "sexual revolution." *Yeah, right!* As long as you didn't end up preggers, then it was *your* problem, and they couldn't be bothered.

I loved the music back then, but I have to say that having women on equal footing with the men nowadays is much more interesting. Joni, when she went "over the pond," had them all shaking in their velvet boots! They couldn't handle the idea of a chick who could *write*, *play*, and *sing*, and she didn't even need a *band behind her.* She was also a hell of an artist and painter—kind of an idol of mine whom I tried to emulate.

I have an uncanny sense of timing for cooking. I know the right moment to start, as I keep my finger on the pulse of the party, if you will. I have made so many of my specialties over the years that I know exactly how long it will take and how long to wait before serving.

I was right on the mark, as the aromas that were wafting from the giant old kitchen (woodburning stove too, mind you) had the guests streaming toward the origin of the pungent smells like moths to a flame! Very gratifying. There is a certain feeling of power in getting famous people do what you want so easily.

The appetizer course was just for starters! I had made arrangements before I arrived to find a fantastic butcher shop that was third generation, only a few kilometers from the estate. I told him it was a bizarre request from the beginning, but he was game and hip from the get-go and was well acquainted with the "master of the realm." I had a car swing round and pick up the thirty pounds of liver Patty, and he had done just as I asked. It had been ground three times to a paste-like consistency. My only problem was finding one of the young maidens at the party to volunteer for my experiment. I was astonished that when we put the word out, they came flocking to the kitchen and *fighting* over whom I would pick! The assignment? I needed someone to lie on their side, naked, so I could completely cover them, from the waist down, in Pat-ay, and the mixture would end up as a mermaid's tail. I had her shower and lie down on the large wooden table. I had to have her skin wet so the mixture would adhere. I fashioned two hollowed-out kumquats, applied mayonnaise to the insides, and used them as "pasties" for her breasts. They worked fantastic! I wove flowers into her hair from the garden, complete with ivy vines and a cherry for her navel. The mermaid's tail was even worked with a fish-scale pattern, using kitchen utensils, carving just like soft clay.

It took about two hours from start to finish. I was *extremely* pleased with my handiwork, and how I posted some kitchen helpers to stand guard so that no one could peek until I was fully ready.

I adjusted the lighting and had plenty of lit candles and bid the revelers to come and get it.

This, I must say, was a party that is *still* talked about today. My pièce de résistance to that point!

Here are the recipes you could duplicate at your own party and create some historic memories of your own. I swear to you, people will be speechless!

Fiery Eggplant Bruschetta

Cut in half 2 large eggplants. Scoop out the pulp and chop. Save the "shells" of the eggplant for serving. Douse chopped eggplant with lemon juice, and set aside. Fry 4 strips of bacon until crispy; set aside. Add to the bacon fat chopped onion and chopped green bell pepper. Add eggplant, diced celery, tomato paste, and a bit of water, 7 cloves of garlic (chopped), extravirgin olive oil, 4 chopped chilis, a good sprinkle of red pepper flakes, a splash of vinegar, some salt, pepper, and a sprinkle of sugar. It should be cooked thoroughly and should be very thick.

Stuff the "shells" with the mixture, and whatever is left over, put it in small bowls. Serve with nan bread fresh from the oven. Break the bread apart, and spoon on the mixture. Excellent with a good red wine.

Nan Bread

Scald ½ cup of milk. Add 1 cup of boiling water, and cool it a bit. Add 2 teaspoon of melted butter, and 2 teaspoon of salt and sugar. Measure into a large mixing bowl: 4 cups of flour and 2 teaspoon each of baking soda and baking powder. Mix well and add just a bit more salt and sugar; mix one last time. Form a dough.

Flour the table top and knead a bit. Shape and *flatten* it. Bake in a hot oven on a stone, if you have one, until very brown. Serve with eggplant.

Liver Pat-Tay Mermaid's Tail

You will need two kumquats, mayo, a cherry, various flowers and vines, and 30 pounds of finely ground liver sausage. *Do not be afraid!* This will make a party *none* of your guests will *ever* forget. You will need large plastic tubs.

30 Pounds Cooked Liver Sausage

Blend with 20 cans of condensed cream of tomato soup. Dissolve 4 cups of gelatin in 7 cups of cold water. Bring the gelatin and water to a boil adding 10 cans of consommé. Bring to boil and turn off and cool. Add to the remaining 2 cups of Worcestershire, 2 cups of salt, 30 cloves of chopped garlic, and 2 cups of chopped parsley. *Blend* all this very well, and shape it, handfuls at a time, onto the model's body and form the mermaid's tail, inscribing with fish scales and the finned tail.

Hollow out your kumquats, and apply with mayo to her breasts. Fashion her hair with the flowers and vines. Please be advised that you will probably have to become *very* stern with the model to not be laughing and giggling the whole time. My model finally got the message and realized the importance of going along with the plan. Let the guests serve themselves with crackers that they scrape up the liver with, and make sure there is plenty of ice-cold beer.

When you see the veneer of liver is running "thin," whisk the guests *away*, and cover the poor girl with a blanket. *Bon appétit!*

CHAPTER THREE

As my reputation spread and I started to become known in the music circles, I acquired another nickname: The Queen of the Munchies. If you are from the '60s, *you know what the munchies are*. 'Nuff said. One of my all-time favorite things to make for people very late at night, when they are *craving* something crunchy, salty, sweet, smooth, and mind-boggling, is *my* version of the very popular snack you used to be able to buy in a box in stores in Southern California known as Screaming Yellow Zonkers.

Remember those? I distinctly remember going to see *2001: A Space Odyssey*, with my boyfriend, when I was fifteen, and we were toasted. I brought a box of Screaming Yellow Zonkers smuggled under my coat. My boyfriend went *wild* on them! I will always remember laughing my ass off as we walked out into the light of the lobby, as he had like eight of them sticking to his cashmere sweater, and he didn't know it! I thought I was going to piss myself!

Here is my version of Screaming Yellow Zonkers.

Pop a bunch of popcorn, removing any that haven't popped. I learned this the hard way when someone cracked a tooth. Have a large flat cookie sheet or two, depending on how much you make. You can go wild on this stuff. In a large saucepan, add 2 cups of regular sugar. Add enough water to be able to stir it, and it is kind of thick. You are going to cook this until it caramelizes and starts to turn brown. When it does, you are going to add a touch of cream and a good nub of butter, keep stirring, add 1 cup of nuts, or more, like walnuts, pecans, and hazelnuts. Make sure it's pourable so if it's too thick, thin it out a little with cream or water.

Stir until you are ready to pour it. Make a layer of popcorn on the greased cookie sheet.

Pour the mixture all over the corn, and put it in the fridge to harden. Take it out and let it reach room temperature and bust it apart with your hands into chunks about 2 inches by 2 inches. Keep it in a container for a long time if you keep it in the fridge. *Beware*, I am warning you, this is a *bona-fide munchie*. It can be devastating to any kind of diet. *Forget about diet!*

OK, here is another late-night munchie that the British love to have with their "spot of tea."

Simple Raspberry Jam Turnovers with Hot Chocolate Sauce

Make a basic pie dough, or if you are too freaked out to make it, go buy it at a store.

You can get a package that has *two* pie doughs. That should almost be enough. Most people have to eat four of these at one time. It's pathetic to watch.

Use the edge of a teacup (the mouth part) to cut large-ish *rounds* of dough.

Spread with raspberry jam on one side, not too much, or it will gush out the sides, and that is so very un-British. Sprinkle with cinnamon and a bit of sugar, fold over, and seal with a fork all around the edge so nothing can escape. Sprinkle with a bit more cinnamon on top, and poke a couple of holes in the top. Brush the outsides with melted butter, and place in a 350-degree oven. While the turnovers are baking, melt a bunch of chocolate in a double-boiler pan (that's a pan with boiling water under and a pan on top, where you melt the chocolate).

When the turnovers are brown, remove and slightly cool. Serve with a bowl of melted chocolate for *dipping*! This can be very messy and can be, in certain circles, a prelude to amorous adventures, just sayin'.

Believe me, times weren't always fun and games and peace and love.

It was a nomadic life at best and filled with uncertainty all the time. You definitely could "get by with a little help from your friends," but not always. Sometimes, during dry spells between gigs, you literally did not know where to go or whom to turn to for a roof over your head. Lorraine had money, so she kept a little apartment in Los Angeles near the Ventura Freeway. It was one of those Jetsons' type of spots with the brightly colored space-age plastic furniture and the big pointy roof to the office.

It had a pool, which was absolutely great, because they knew me there and I could swim any time I wanted, but I couldn't stay there unless I paid. I did not have the luxury of not worrying about money.

During these dry spells, I found myself back to cleaning homes of people who were on the road. I got a call at the ramshackle spot on Ridgedale Trail, where I got my mail and phone calls, and was told that Sebastian would be flying in within a few days and he wondered if I might go over and tidy up, as he was bringing a guest. He had been out of town for about a month. I headed over to Topanga in my beat-up VW bug convertible with all my cleaning stuff. I could carry everything I needed in two plastic buckets. I found the key under the big, fat Buddha in the garden and opened the door. As soon as I entered, I was struck in the face by this horrible, acrid, slightly sweet, sickening smell! I had, earlier in the morning, sprayed myself with some Shalimar perfume and had to pull my shirt up over my nose to keep from puking. It immediately dawned on me that it was the smell of a human in filthy clothes who hadn't bathed in a very long time. The houses in the canyons did not have any type of security back then, and it was fairly easy to break in. I heard some muttering and shuffling in the bedroom behind the door, and I immediately pulled out my marine flare gun (yes, like the ones people use on boats to shoot signal flares up into the sky). It was the perfect weapon, since you did not need a license or a permit. I kept it in my poke when I was in Los Angeles. The door opened, and there he was! My first impression was that he was rather Manson-esque with his wild hair and wild eyes, but I knew he had just recently gone to prison for a very long time, so this guy couldn't be him.

His clothes were literally rags, and his aroma was enough to knock you off your feet. I pointed the flare gun at him and began my speech: "I don't know who you are, but you do not belong here, and I am very sorry, but you are going to have to leave right now. I do not want to call the police, so please leave. This weapon I have is a flare gun. If I were to shoot you, the flare would enter your body and burn a hole in you that would be about a foot in diameter and would burn at three thousand degrees! It would kill you." He did not say a single word the whole time. He just shambled toward the door and split.

He took nothing with him. I spent the *whole* day there, disinfecting *every* single surface in that whole place. It was a disgusting mess, but I left there knowing it was "ship shape and Bristol fashion."

I even left a bottle of wine and some cheese and crackers for Sebastian and his guest. I never told him about the incident, since I knew he led a very high-stress life, and all it would do would be to cause him to worry himself sick each time he left for more than a day or two.

Not too long after this happened, Lorraine came back into town, depressed and unusually quiet and somber. I instantly knew something was up. Her mercurial relationship with her ex, Jean-Paul, had deteriorated to the point that all they ever did was *fight*. He did continue to send her money every month, as he did for his three other ex-wives, but every time they were together, there would always be an argument. We got together the first night and got drunk and smoked some pot, and I did my usual to boost her spirits and try to convince her everything was going to be OK. I awoke with the sun and had work planned for that day, and she *never* got up in the morning, *ever*! I left as quietly as I could, with her snoring away.

Two days later (I had been busy), I dropped by to see if she was still there. All the curtains were closed, as I had left them. It was dark; the light from the door showed that she was lying on the floor. It was about two in the afternoon, and she was naked. I opened up all the curtains and checked her over; she was breathing, but she had a funny color on the face. I wrapped her in a bathrobe and called the office to have them send an ambulance right away. I placed a wet washcloth on her forehead and checked inside her mouth to see if there was anything in there. At this point, she was moaning but didn't open her eyes. I tried to pick her off the floor, but she started waving her arms around, and it was impossible, so I left her where she was. Within a couple of minutes, the ambulance took her to Hollywood Presbyterian emergency. I stayed and waited. They pumped her stomach.

When I knew that she would live, I left. She was incredibly fortunate! It wasn't until much later that I learned that she had an especially bad row with Jean-Paul and felt like a hypocrite taking his money, even though they were not married anymore. She sank into a black hole of depression, and it was compounded because she found out that I was the *only* person who realized she was MIA and went to check on her. She had taken twenty Tuinals. It would have killed anyone else. She was a scrappy and tough survivor. I brought her along with me on my go-arounds and errands for the next week, after she got out of the hospital, so I could keep an eye on her. She eventually popped back up and was her usual ebullient, chatty self, talking big plans.

About three months earlier than all this, she told me about an upcoming trip to the Caribbean.

One of Jean-Paul's old bandmates had a wooden sailboat, which was gorgeous and immaculately well cared for. It had been custom-built for a senator in the '50s and was eighty feet at the waterline. I believe they called it a sloop. I got the invitation to go along and be the galley chef for the trip.

I was *really* looking forward to it, as I had never cooked in a ship or sailboat galley, and it seemed like a great challenge. We would be going when the weather was perfect, the boat being moored in Florida year-round, and not in hurricane season. It was still a ways off, and we had a couple more months to plan for it. There would be seven people, besides Lorraine and myself. Neither of us knew anything about sailing, but the owner/skipper had sailed to many exotic locales like the Marquesas and Fiji and to the Big Island, Hawaii. We had no qualms about going.

I knew the voyage was looming, but the dry spell ended, and we were as busy as ever!

This time, it was to the East Coast for a Black Sunday concert and backstage party at Madison Square Garden. This band was along the lines of Alice Cropper, with all the severed doll heads and blood. *Not* my cup of tea, but *whatever.* I drew the line at requests for any type of blood, or offal, or "organ meats"! I came up with a novel idea. I had been introduced to an incredible recipe from a very close friend who said his grama in Oklahoma had been making it ever since he was a young boy and he was always recruited to help her with it. It was great, because this recipe only required that it be kept *ice-cold.*

I did not have to request any special situation for *cooking* backstage.

Here is what I made for the after concert party:

Dutch Lunch or Steak Tartare

2 cherry tomatoes
4–5 pounds of raw, finely chopped *lean* top-quality steak
10 dill pickles juice of four lemons
4 raw eggs (*fresh!*)
1 handful of salt
1 handful of red cayenne pepper (yes, a handful!)
2 cups of finely chopped onion
8 mashed anchovies
3 finely chopped tomatoes
2 jars of capers (drained)
1 whole head of parsley
5 sprigs of fresh thyme, stripped of stems
1 bottle of Worcestershire sauce
1 small bottle of extravirgin olive oil
1 handful of coarse ground pepper

Chop all this with a sharp cleaver or knife. Chop, chop, chop, chop, chop. When you get tired, have someone else take over. The *whole mess* needs to be chopped super fine so that *all* the ingredients are melded totally.

Have a prepared tray, lined with parchment paper or tin foil, and mound the mixture into two equal amounts that are shaped as female breasts. Top each mound with a cherry tomato.

Serve with small squares of pumpernickel bread and ice-cold dark beer! Need I say that this was a *big hit* with all the *guys*! As an added treat for these British rockers, I brought along one of my English specialties, which I called Keith's shepherd pie. He was always spouting off about how his was the best, as he "learned" it from his mom. I feel mine was far superior since I used a *real* pastry crust and added *three* cheeses to the mashed-potato topping!

Here is Keith's shepherd pie.

Prepare a *large* baking dish with butter or oil.

Place your crust into the bottom, making sure to push it all the way into the side of the dish. Poke a few holes in the bottom with a fork. Shape the edge and use the fork tines to make a pattern all around the edge.

Bake in a 350-degree oven until it starts to brown. Remove from oven.

In a *large* skillet, brown ground sirloin beef, with onions, peas, carrots, and mushrooms. Salt and pepper it, and add some dried thyme and soy sauce to flavor the mixture.

Make a batch of mashed potatoes. Grate some cheddar and Monterey Jack cheese, and whisk into the mash with some cream and butter and salt and pepper.

Pour the meat mixture into the baked pie crust, making sure to drain *all* liquid!

Top with the potato mixture and sprinkle with grated Parmesan cheese and paprika, and bake until the topping is crusty and brown. I guarantee this will give you complete satisfaction!

Lorraine in Switzerland while living with Fernando.

Looking out the galley window on Caribbean sailing trip

Me, taking a break from cooking in the galley

a Caribbean sunrise

Colin and I

Colin Archer teaching me “archery”!!

one of our wedding anniversaries

me on St. Thomas USVI

wearing a dress I made for my wedding

Colin and I on holiday

Goofing around

Wedding Bells

my trusty ukulele from the time I was a kid

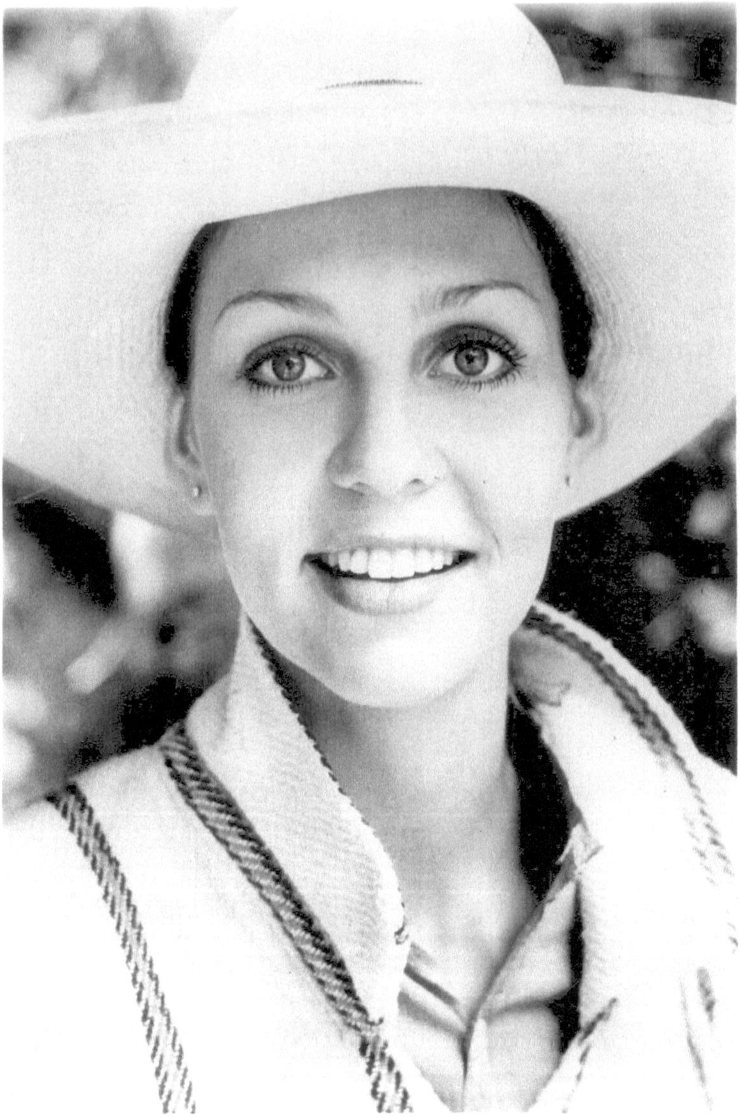

LORRAINE MASON

Lorraine in her model days at Nina Blanchard

view of the bay where we stayed on St. Thomas

some of our fresh fish that we caught along the way

sailing

yacht club

dinner "down below", cooked by yours truly

yacht club bar

jungle trail on St. Thomas

our sailing buddies, Howie, Jo Ann, and their kids

their sailboat

the dining area off the galley

more sailing friends

yacht club

hanging laundry out to dry- out at sea

me, with colin's Gibson

on the island

promo shot of me for my business

When I met Colin at Big Sur

Lorraine and Fernando in Switzerland

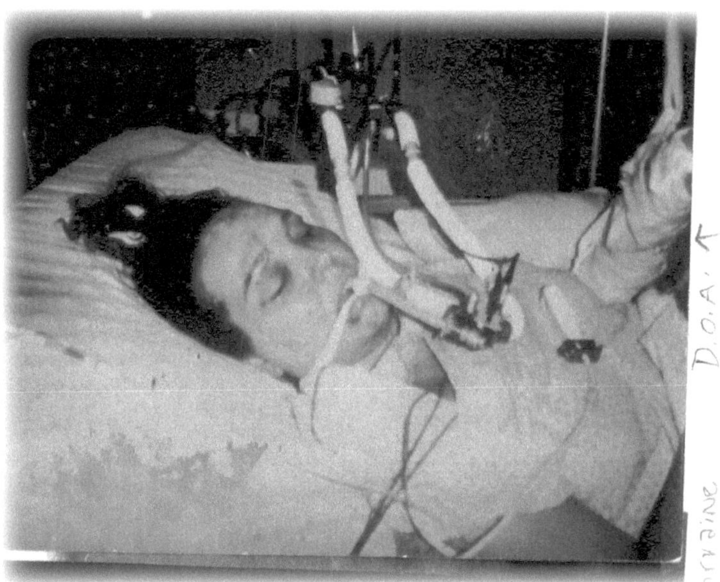

Lorraine, pronounced D.O.A. after her horrifying car accident. She barely survived and endured 26 surgeries during the rest of her life.

goofing around between gigs, in Laurel Canyon

Beer shampoo

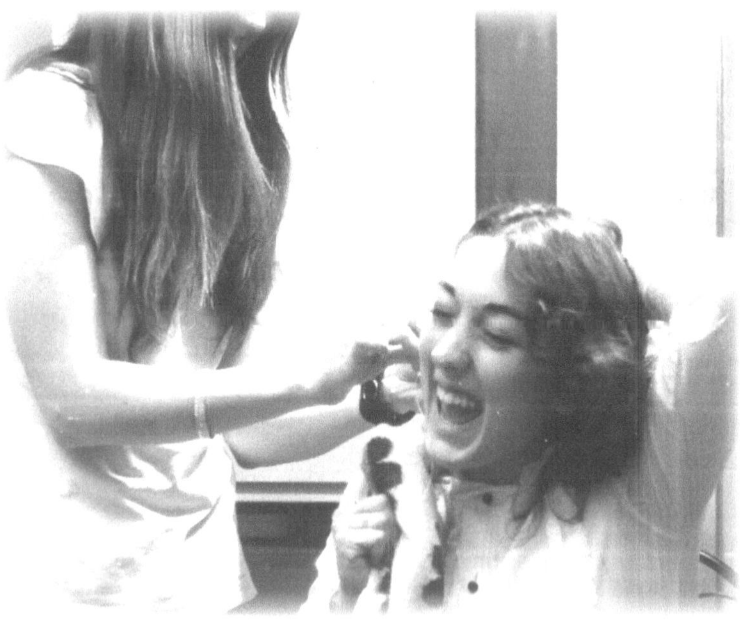

I pierced ears to make money too...........

A cake I made for an after concert backstage party.
I cut an orange in half to made the "boobs'".

the place in Laurel Canyon where I stayed when I had no where else to go. That's me "clowning around"

Hiking a trail with Colin in the woods of Laurel Canyon

CHAPTER FOUR

Before I knew it, the Caribbean trip was looming just on the horizon. We didn't need to prepare very much as we had a place in Miami that we could get clothes from and whatever we needed for the voyage. We just brought our essentials. For me, it was my poke, and for Lorraine, it was her jewelry and her special bathing suits, etc.

It was September, and when we arrived in Miami, the weather was just perfect, in the upper seventies. The owner/skipper with the incredible singing voice took us to where the sloop was moored. I was *knocked out.* This sailboat was stunning. The *whole* thing was wood except for the hull, which was white. Everywhere you looked, the wood was gleaming and highly polished. There would be plenty of room for all nine of us. I got to check out the galley, and there was ample room to store everything and to move around and cook, and there was even a nice seating area right off the cooking area.

As I have mentioned before, I knew absolutely *nothing* about sailing. As a child growing up, I was used to being out on the ocean, as one of my uncles had a fine fishing vessel and my dad and four brothers were obsessed with fishing. It was a good thing, because our freezer was always packed with locally caught halibut, barracuda, surf perch, skate, and shark. My mom taught me how to make exceptional dishes with all these fish. Since we were strapped for money most of the time, this was a welcome bounty from the sea. On a few trips, I would get to go, because I loved fishing too!

I usually caught something, each and every time I was allowed to go out. I realized from a young age that I never experienced seasickness. As our sailing excursion to the Caribbean was getting closer, I was hopeful that I would not experience any seasickness at all, but I had never gone on a trip of 1,100 miles in the Atlantic before either. I would just have to wait and see. Once I had met with the owner/skipper and got to take the tour, a few of my fears were allayed.

The sailboat was definitely big enough that nine people would not be cramped together. I started thinking that what would one do if they just could not stand the other people, and there was bickering or arguing or fighting on such a trip. What if the people just did not gel? As departure got closer and closer, I started to understand and fully realize what a huge undertaking this was going to be, and everyone was placing their confidence in *me* to provide one of the most important aspects of a two-week trip out on the open ocean: their *meals*! I made a vow to myself that I was going to get the absolute *most* out of this, and I would learn every single thing I could about being a galley chef *and* about sailing. My first day of checking out *The Mystere*, I learned, at least, about portside, starboard side, the giant, solid wood, single mast of a sloop and the boom. At certain times, there would also be a sail that was run called a jib, and it was usually *very* brightly colored with extravagant designs or patterns of sailcloth. The owner explained to me that because we were taking this trip in September, whoever wanted to fish along the way would be more than welcome, as it was a perfect time to catch billfish (twelve to fourteen days before a full moon). Fishing at night was very good, and one could catch yellowfin tuna (year round) and red grouper. He explained that there were a lot of lionfish that were considered dangerous and poisonous. He said that if one caught a red grouper in the Caribbean waters (they were coral feeders) and brought it out of the water, he or she would see that the grouper had bright-blue dots on its body against the bright-red color but that the blue dots would quickly fade, after it was out of the water for any length of time.

I set about trying to do research on how to properly cook all these tropical-water fish that we might be lucky enough to catch along our way. After I got my bearings, once I actually got to see where I would be working, and Lorraine had the chance to scope out the most awesome and largest berth for her resplendent self to dwell (I informed her that the *owner* would probably have the most spacious bedroom!), I left with notes I had taken down and set about making my master list of what I would need. I figured on the fact that I would be responsible for nine people, for three meals a day, for approximately two weeks, wow. I also made a plan to stash some things in hidden places, in case the larder ran unexpectedly low before we arrived at Saint Thomas.

Here is my list for stocking the galley—jerky (it can be hydrated with hot water and chopped to add to salads), lots of Top Ramen dry noodles, dried coconut milk, Italian dry salami, hard cheeses, dry tack crackers, canned condensed milk, coffee, tea, sugar, jarred tartar sauce, large canned hams, cabbage, carrots, potatoes, onions, all forms of citrus (lemons, limes, oranges for vitamin C—*no* scurvy on this voyage!), apples, trail mix and granola, nuts, dried fruit, cans of Spam (vegetarians nightmare!), jars of jam, peanut butter, flour (since I would make bread on board), spices, condiments, oil, garlic, candy bars, canned tuna, jars of mayo, canned coconut milk, and various seeds like alfalfa, mung beans, etc., to make fresh green sprouts at sea, for some greens. Jarred salsa, chips, bottle juices, charcoal for the onboard BBQ, dry beans like pinto, white beans, dry split peas, large boxes of oats, raisins, pasta, bottled marinara sauce, cans of green chilis, powdered eggs, dry biscotti, cans of sardines, cans of salmon, canned shrimp, Tabasco, soy sauce, 4 bottles of good whiskey, tons of wine, tons of beer, and *tons* of water.

Oh, and I made a note to bring my Hawaiian ukelele I got when I was fifteen years old at a thrift store for three dollars. Over the years, I taught myself how to play a few old standards like "I'll see you in my dreams" (I know this was one of George Harrison's all-time favorites, and he played it quite a bit for friends at dinner parties). It had really come in handy for me a few times to liven up bored hotel guests and dinner parties that had gone flat.

When we returned home to Los Angeles, I had a very good sense of what was coming, and I started to realize that things could go wrong. When I got to Ridgedale Trail, I actually sat down, in the quiet, by myself, and wrote out a will and testament. I would leave it with one of my good friends. Taking assessment of my life and what I would have left if I were to somehow *die*, I realized there wasn't much!

My two younger sisters might fight over who got the beat-up VW bug, but that was about it. I cheerfully convinced myself that my security would follow soon. I busied myself, with the time remaining, by tying up a bunch of loose ends and soliciting the help of various girlfriends I could trust to fill in the gaps. I told them what was left of my family, what I was doing, and when I should be returning. My sister Carol and I were very close. I told her not to get freaked out if I was a few days late, as you can never pinpoint sailing excursions. I told her I would contact her on Maui, when I got back to Los Angeles.

With only a couple days to spare, the brunt of what I had consigned to and my lying to the owner, Rej, about my "vast "experience, began to play tricks on me. Egads, I had to prepare three meals a day for nine people for possibly thirteen days! *None of whom I knew!* I tried as best I could to calm myself and try to take the approach I had *always* used: "Just see how it goes. You're smart—you'll figure out whatever comes along." One great thing about the trip was that Rej was only going one way. He was simply moving the sailboat from Miami to the US Virgin Islands, where the boat would be residing for the next year. So all of us would be flying back to Miami after the one leg of the trip. I *really* warmed up to that idea! Lorraine got her invite (and me too) from Rej, as she was thinking of getting a place *very* close to Jean Paul's two ex-wives, who already lived there. All three of JP's ex-ladies were grand friends! One of the wives lived only eight houses away from the other.

JP took care of them financially, and having a sailboat of his own that he kept moored in the Virgin Islands made for a certain weird "camaraderie" between them all, as they would take care of things for him when he visited once or twice a year—to earn their keep? Who knows. It was 1971! I think JP *really* liked the idea of having his own little "Virgin Island harem."

Lorraine thought it could work for her too. She would check it out and feel the water, so to speak.

I had everyone's name written down with a short description, just so I could get used to them all and not look like a fool and forget. There was Rej, Lorraine and I, Steven and David (from the band), Neil and Sasha (the passionate, trust-fund, hedonistic couple), and Denny and Michelle (who were brother and sister). In all, there would be four expert sailors, and for a boat the size of Rej's, that was cutting it close, but they had all experienced long sailing voyages on similar-size vessels. I was interested and wanted to learn, so maybe I could help out, or at least, I was hopeful. I learned that once we were under way, someone would be doing an eight-hour shift, every eight hours, so three times a day, the watch would change. This meant that besides the three meals a day for nine people, I would be bringing a sandwich and coffee to the person on watch. There was *so* much to know and prepare for that it was mind-boggling.

While I had prepared and stocked what I thought was necessary and got used to everything in the galley being "gimbled." *Gimble shelves*, etc., means that everything stays upright as the boat is leaning from side to side. The stove was *not* on a gimble, but it had a curious tall "lip" at the edge. That is because if you were not being attentive, the pot you were cooking with could *slide off.* You could be seriously burned, and it would be quite a disastrous mess. There was also a gimble BBQ back at the transom. This sailboat had been retrofitted with a small fridge and had an oven, which was a real advantage to some sailboats that had the bare necessities at best.

There were two heads, but we would be using "solar shower bags," hung outside, filled with fresh water that would be warmed by the sun for taking showers. Upon my first inspection, I found that there was a very tight cubbyhole, with a padded cushion bench that was private, and it was right off the galley, so I picked that for my "berth." The cushion lid opened up for stowage, so I could put all my gear under my bunk. I tried it out while I was there, and it was fine for sleeping, with a couple of good pillows, which I brought.

I was so busy with my job inside that I never dreamed of the "machinations" going on behind the scenes for the technical side of the trip. I was told that when you went on a trip out in the wilderness, for example, you *always* had a backup for something, *always.* This was a military concept too. When you went on a long sea voyage, you were to have a backup for your backup, for your backup. No room for errors. Your life could depend on something as simple as a very long steel cable and a shiny gold hook. The *sea* is a *harsh mistress*. The course had to be plotted and all the equipment in excellent working order. There was a huge checklist that had to be gone through and gone through again. If we hit "dead calms," there was an auxiliary motor that was in excellent condition.

The estimated time of departure was 9:00 a.m. the following day, September 6, 1971. We stayed at a nearby motel.

Lorraine and I did not party like usual the night before. We were "good" and got to bed early and had had only a glass or two of wine. We took a cab over to where the boat was moored. We were *early*! Lorraine had never been early in her life; it was because of me. We were both giddy with excitement, and I was a little queasy. I hoped it wasn't a harbinger of stomach problems to come! By 10:00 a.m., everyone was assembled *except* the trust-fund brats. Rej said that he had only allotted so much time for them to be late and if they weren't there, we would leave without them! I knew he would cut Neil a little more slack, since he was a sailor also, but did not have the expert experience of Rej, Steven, David, and Denny. Just before we cast off, Rej announced that if *anyone* thought they could smuggle *any* kind of illegal substance, there would be serious repercussions and that all of us could end up in jail for a very long time! Everyone said they were not carrying. We got under way at 1:00 p.m.! It did not bode well for the beginning, but at least, we had a gorgeous day with light winds, perfect for our takeoff.

There was a flurry of activity, and before we knew it, we were quite a ways out. No one really wanted anything, until around sunset. I had planned for this first night and set out a very nice platter of cheeses, crackers, charcuterie, some diced devilled eggs, and a spot of caviar, and we popped some champagne. As I happened to glance backward, I noticed the lights of Miami fading away, and I had the queerest feeling. I had never felt anything like that feeling before. A feeling of loneliness? I couldn't put my finger on it.

As Rej had his little powwow with us all as we all finally assembled, he made us form a circle and join hands. We were all checking each other out and sizing each other up. Rej said, "We are all bound on this experience by our mutual love of music. I know that we will do well together and become lifelong friends after the fact. May we have a trip that we can all look back on with fond memories."

Rej was in his forties, with a bit of gray on his temples. He wore his hair long, as all the other guys on board. He had made the bulk of his fortunes as a stock trader but got to the point where he realized he wasn't living his passion. He moved lock, stock, and barrel to the West Coast and set up shop as a band promoter and a concert promoter. He had enough money to play around until he could learn the ropes. Eventually, he had a stable of bands he was very proud to promote. He used a novel approach, by letting the bands have a *lot* of say in the management and financial gain, which was unusual at the time. Rej was already wealthy; he was doing it because he loved the music and the process.

It was funny that at the time, we thought of him as a kind of father figure, since the rest of us were in our late teens or early twenties. He was still a kid by today's standards!

Steven and David were from one of the bands that Rej managed. Everyone mutually benefitted from the liaison because they were one of the hottest acts during the last of the sixties and the beginning of the seventies, having a smash album right out of the gates, with a follow-up that was at the top of the charts for over a year. They were taking a well deserved break on this sail. Steven was light haired, and David was dark haired. They were not dressed in sailing garb when they arrived, instead wearing plaid shirts, jeans, and Sperry Top-Siders. None of us were sporting sailing gear! Footwear was a big deal because of the boat and safety, so at least, we all were wearing the proper footgear.

Neil and Sasha were a story unto themselves. They were from extreme wealth and had never had to have a job of any sort. They were what we called trust-fund babies. At least Neil knew *something* of sailing, and Rej was hoping to put him to work. He was very thin and actually quite effeminate.

His ribs stuck out from his slightly sunken chest. He had *no* tan. She was delicate, blond, with very dark roots, a total amalgam of hippie chic of the day. She probably brought more clothes than Lorraine! She was about 5'4" and seemed almost totally helpless. They were there to have a great time and had no desires to do anything to assist the rest of us in any way. I think their whole lives must have been that way to that point.

Denny and Michelle, on the other hand, were hardy, strapping Southern California beach kids. He was three years older than she, and they came from a middle-class family in the San Fernando Valley. Their dad had a regular job and supported his wife and four kids. They both left home at an early age, much as I had done, to seek their fortunes in the music biz. He played guitar, she sang, and they got gigs from time to time all around the Southland. They were on this trip because they had heard about it from Steven, and they just wanted the experience, as Denny had crewed on a large catamaran called *The Sea Smoke*, which sailed from Los Angeles to the Big Island. He picked it up very quickly. I liked them from the get-go. They were beautiful and down-to-earth, and there was no BS with either of them. They were always *up* for whatever was going down.

Unfortunately, by the second day and the swells were a little bigger as we got farther out from land, Sasha developed seasickness and retired below. It wasn't bad at first, just nausea and a bit of vomiting, but we convinced her that being below was the worst thing she could do and it would only compound the problem. We convinced her that fresh air and being up on deck would help and for her to keep her eye on the horizon so as to minimize the up and down motion of the swells. She was the only one of all of us who suffered almost the whole way. She would be OK one day and ill the next. It did not help matters that by now, you could see *no* land anywhere you looked. It even spooked me, but I had too much to do to even think about it.

I had read enough books (I was an avid reader) through my years to know all about people who had been lost at sea for months at a time and how they had to survive in life rafts by catching fish and birds and capturing rainwater in buckets and how they would be constipated for weeks on end because of the lack of fiber or fruit in their diets, only to be rescued by a stray fishing vessel when they were merely weeks from their demise, having lost half of their body weight, so it wasn't lost on me—*all* the things that could go wrong. But I was convinced of Rej's prowess and knowledge and expert seamanship that I was able to allay my fears. I had read how in a raging storm a large sailboat could literally roll over, break off the mast, and *go down* in approximately five minutes! That wasn't going to happen to us!

The mere fact that he had the presence of mind to make sure we left in the first week of September made me feel secure, knowing that you *never* want to attempt that voyage in the Atlantic, anywhere near the dreaded hurricane season, which officially starts the first few days of November. To go then could be suicide, no matter how expert you were!

I settled into a routine whereby I realized that it would be easier to put together three things for the meals and set it out, buffet style, so people could take what they wanted or mix all three things together if they wished. I was so glad I brought a little alarm clock I stowed away with my pillows, because I was *always* up before anyone else. I would make oatmeal, set out box cereal, a large bowl of trail mix, and a large bowl of granola with nuts and cinnamon and spices, and of course, *coffee* and bottled juices. This worked out very well for the breakfast situation. Once I got the coffee going, I loved going up on the deck and watching the spectacular sunrises. If it was a little rough out and especially windy, it was always a good idea to wear a harness and be "clipped on." If a person went overboard and you were travelling at a speed of seven to ten knots, it was *bye-bye*, as there was *no* way they could come back and get you, plus even if they could, you would be so hyperthermic you wouldn't survive. I learned a *lot*. I learned about the single-masted sloop and how it could run many other types of sails besides the main sail; you could run a variety of sails depending on the wind, like you could run two sails at one time; there were jibs, like a genny, or genoa, or a storm jib, like a "mule," which is a small jib and can be run as the *only* sail in *really* high wind. A spinnaker was usually wild colors and patterns that you would hoist when you were "running with the wind," and the material was either half ounce, or you could switch to an ounce and a half. You could hit a dead calm anywhere on the seas, but it was always a good idea to have an auxiliary motor, which we had.

On the third day, the most amazing thing happened! David was not on watch and was using the heavy-duty fishing gear and landed a twenty-five pound red grouper! It was the most incredible fish I had ever seen. It was bright red but had dazzling, glowing blue spots *all* over the body. As it was exposed to the air, it rapidly lost the blue spots. The fish was gutted and cleaned and perfectly filleted. *I went to work for dinner!*

Here is what I did with that gorgeous fish:

Red Caribbean Grouper with Potatoes and Peppers

In a large, high-sided pan, heat olive oil. Add 5 cups of cubed potatoes, 2 each of red, green, and yellow bell peppers (cubed), 5 sprigs thyme or dried, one can of tomato paste. Stir around. Add 2 cups of chopped onion. Stir again. Season with salt and pepper and a handful of red chili pepper flakes.

If you have some butter, add a large pat. Let it melt into the mixture. Pour in 1 full bottle of white wine and 3 cups of chicken stock, made from bouillon cubes. Stir well and add 5 crushed cloves of garlic. Stir again and cover with a lid. Simmer until potatoes are still firm but cooked through. Cut your fish fillets into large chunks. *Carefully* nestle them into the stew so they are completely covered up. *Do not stir anymore.* Just shake the pan. You do not want the fish to break apart—cover until fish is done. Do *not* overcook it. Ladle into bowls. Drizzle each portion with a bit of olive oil so it looks gleaming. Sprinkle each bowl with a bit of dried thyme.

Serve with a chilled white wine like Pinot Grigio, and bread if you have it.

It was spectacular, if I say so myself, and after that meal, Rej had *no* qualms about my being a true galley chef. I had totally proved myself to one and all. Loraine said I was beaming.

The only person who could not partake was poor Sasha. Even a whiff of fish sent her reeling. She stuck to bland things like cereal and tea. You could tell she was already losing weight.

On the second day, the stew had time for the flavors to really meld together, and it was even better the second time around, once it had been heated up again. Grouper turns white and fluffy when cooked. It has a sweet, delicate taste. It reminded me somewhat of halibut.

All the dark scenarios that I had floating around my head about ill-fated sailing trips were starting to ease as we entered our fifth day, and everything and everybody was on cruise or autopilot. It was nice to look out the galley window and see other bits of land and other islands it made one feel like you weren't exactly at the ends of the earth on an endless sea.

I had finished up with breakfast and had cleaned everything and put it all away, so I went up on deck for a bit. Steven was doing his watch, and he was still hungry, so I took him a cup of tea and a sandwich. With other islands in sight, it was not unusual to see the odd bird here or there.

We were clipping along with brisk wind, and I caught a bit of a chill, so I decided to go back below and begin prep for the next meal. I was doing a batch of chili and green pepper corn bread for lunch. As I got down the steps and turned, I was hit smack in the face by the sight of Neil and Sasha *in flagrante on the dining table*! I was speechless and managed to sputter "Geeze, and we're supposed to *eat* on this table!" They snapped to attention and started making moves to cover their exposed areas. I was further astounded to see that our own scrawny Neil had been favored by Mother Nature in a certain spot. You *go*, Sasha girl!

She must have gotten a second wind from her seasickness to be so athletic. We all busted out laughing at my asinine comment, and we all shared a drink. That image will be burned in my mind forever, and here I just told of how everything was so smooth and nothing out of the ordinary was happening! I spent a full hour disinfecting the dining area with Lysol, for lunch, which was in a mere three hours. "I won't tell if you won't tell" was what Neil whispered to me as they went up the steps. I would only tell Lorraine, and we had a big guffaw over glasses of wine later.

It was not unusual to go a day without seeing one or more of the people on board. It must have been because of the sheer size of *The Mystere* that we never felt confined or claustrophobic.

What a luxury to be that wealthy. When you have money like that, you probably no longer have to worry about paying bills ever. I wouldn't know; I scraped from month to month and had no money in the bank for a cushion. I really tried to put a little away every chance I got, but some catastrophe would always come along, and her name started with an *L*, and *poof* it would be gone. I am sure I missed out on a major portion of the trip, because I was so focused on my job. Everyone made a special effort to praise my efforts, and I hadn't had a dissatisfied customer to that point. I put my heart and soul into each day and planned everything out in my bunk the night before.

I figured it out that if it took thirteen days to get there (it could possibly only take ten to eleven), I would be making thirty-nine meals for nine people. I needed to keep the *boredom* at bay the best I could. That is why I made a big pot of chili and my killer green chili corn bread for lunch.

The corn bread is really simple, but if you do the changes, it becomes really special.

Corn Bread

Use 2 boxes of ready-made corn-bread mix. Get the kind that only uses water.

Mix well and add 1 cup of shredded sharp cheddar cheese.

Open a can of diced green chilis and drain.

Add the chilis to the mixture, and mix in the cheese and the chilis.

Add 1 teaspoon of powdered cumin and red powdered chili pepper. Mix one last time, and bake in a baking pan in a 350-degree oven till browned on top.

The *aroma* of this baking will bring them running without ringing the chow bell!

I hardly saw Rej, except for meals and just before everyone turned in. He would sometimes have a beer or two with everyone, talk with us, smoke a cigar, and drift to his cabin, which was, of course, the largest and most plush of all the berths.

The sixth day dawned and began routinely at about 10:00 a.m. or so. David was fishing off the transom and hooked into something very large, and sure enough, it came flying out of the water. It was a billfish. When it came fully out of the water, it was apparent that it was *not* a full-grown fish but a young one. The guys decided that if they could dehook it, they would return it to the ocean. They did manage to haul it out onto the deck, but the rig had been swallowed. They cut what they could, being ever mindful of the sword, and flopped it back into the sea.

We also caught a very large lionfish, but there was *no way* I was going to mess with that! They were starting to become a problem in the Caribbean. They were cool to look at but a real nightmare.

Late in the afternoon, I was told by Lorraine that there was a coast-guard-type vessel (looked official) that was about half the length of the sailboat and was coming near us. They got closer and closer, and I did not think anything of it—I just went about my business. They used their bullhorn to speak to Rej, but I could not hear what was going on.

Within five minutes or so, they were heading off and were gone. I did not find out till much later that it scared the piss out of Neil and Sasha, because even after the speech and dressing down Rej gave everyone about *no* illegal substances and how, by God, I would not go to jail for some stupid, infantile, teen prankster's need to break the law, Neil had brought some pot anyway! He and Sasha had to grab big mugs of orange juice and went into the head and *ate it all*. They had to wash mouthfuls of it, down with big gulps of orange juice. Needless to say, they were both *junk* for the next two days and laid low.

Rej never found out about the kitchen orgy or the pot incident. Whew!

He was like our dad, and we were all the bad little kids! This time, what he didn't know wouldn't hurt him. If they had boarded us and found the pot, his whole life could have been in jeopardy. Neil was selfish and wasn't thinking at all.

We had cleared the Bahamas on the sixth day, and we were headed straight out into the Atlantic going east. This would be the farthest out into the Atlantic that we would get before turning southeast. I was told that when we hit seventy degrees west and approximately twenty-five degrees north, we would turn south for a straight shot at the US Virgin Islands.

The northeast trades would be the best part of the trip. I couldn't personally get involved with all this, because I had my hands *full* with the creature comforts of everyone on board, from the time I got up until I dropped into my bunk! I am just relaying the info floating around.

We did hit a couple of pretty good rain squalls in the Atlantic proper, but no big deal.

We crossed the Tropic of Cancer (which I didn't know very much about) and headed south.

Because of the fact that we hadn't encountered any real hardships or unexpected problems, we were estimated to arrive at Saint Thomas in nine days! Our wise leader had chosen a perfect route, one used by seasoned captains who had spent their lifetimes delivering yachts and boats to owners, from Southern Florida to the British and US Virgin Islands. We only had to motor a couple of times and still had plenty of fuel cans lashed down, and we obviously would have provisions left over in the larder. *Not bad!* I think I faked it very well. I was *so* proud of myself.

Not much more to report at this leg of the journey. There had been *no* arguments at all or drunken displays of stupidity. No one fell overboard, and Rej seemed to ease up a bit after we sailed south. We did catch a few more fish, which were dispatched quickly from the BBQ, washed down with beer and wine.

On our last night, I wanted to do something special, and we were informed that we did not want to make port at night, and we would be heaving to to await the dawn. It was fantastic to see the twinkling lights again. I was riding on cloud 10.

I had stashed away a jar of the finest Beluga caviar and a special bottle of Dom Perignon, thanks to Lorraine. I made a platter of melba toast points and broke out my little "horn" spoon for the caviar; some of the crackers, I spooned the caviar onto and adorned with a red pimento. Rej did us the honors by opening the champagne, and we all toasted the captain! Everyone looked beautiful in that light that night, tanned and beaming, rosy cheeks, and glistening eyes. *We had done it*. I broke out my uke and began strumming my old ditty, the only one I knew, and Lorraine began to do a hula dance, and before we knew it, everyone pitched in singing. What a night. I went to bed early, as I knew the next day would be filled with going ashore (getting our land legs back) and doing the customs and immigration dance.

Neil and Sasha announced that they had decided to head over to Saint Croix for an extra week and did not want to fly home. Well, they could afford to do whatever struck their fancy, I guess! Sasha seemed no worse for wear because of the seasickness she suffered through on the first half of the trip. I hardly got to know Denny and Michelle; he was sailing most of the time and then would hit the sack. We spoke only during mealtimes, and Michelle mostly stayed to herself or spent time with Lorraine. We vowed to stay in touch and maybe get together away from the rigors of sailing.

I could not sleep for hours; I was so excited and relieved, reliving the whole experience in my head. Eventually, I drifted off.

I was up before dawn, as I really wanted to see the sun come up on this gorgeous place I had never been. I made coffee and tea for everyone, but no one seemed to want to eat anything. Fine with me! As we all assembled in the galley (the common meeting place), Rej appeared all spiffy and shaved, his long hair groomed. As he did when we departed on the journey, he made a little speech of how proud he was of all of us, what great shipmates we were, what a hell of a job we all did, which made his job easier, and how he would sail again with *any* of us anytime.

He would be mooring his sloop at the Saint Thomas Yacht Club, which he himself had partially helped finance many years earlier in 1964. Within those seven years, it had really grown, with an outdoor patio with tables and chairs, a restaurant that served excellent food and had a bar and even had tennis courts.

The white-trouser, pastel crowd hung out with the sailor crowd, who wore almost nothing, and everyone got along famously. They offered sailing lessons and had little sabots for learning.

It was all quite posh. I talked with Rej privately, and he wholeheartedly agreed to give me a rousing letter of recommendation, which I knew would serve me well in the future! Rej was excited, as his grown son, Ian, would be flying over to join his dad for a week or so. Lorraine and I planned on going home to Los Angeles within two days.

After she looked at a couple of cottages, in the neighborhood where Catya and Dawn lived. There was one that would be coming available very soon, as the tenant was going on an extended world cruise. It was not huge—it had two bedrooms, one bath, and was about twenty feet up, high off the road, with a nice little outdoor patio that was fringed with palms and a *fabulous* ocean view with boats moored in the little bay. All the furniture was white wicker and lots of pastel colors with beachy art prints on the walls. Lorraine wanted it, and Cat and Dawn said they would handle it for her, and they would let her know when to send the money.

Back to our departure from *The Mystere*. All I had was my fringed jacket, my poke, my pillows, my alarm clock, and my little Buddha I had brought and put on a shelf, for good luck. I was always a very light packer, so I could stay mobile at all times. Lorraine had two large bags, but they were manageable. I borrowed her hat. I was wearing sandals, bell-bottom jeans, a bathing-suit top, and her hat. We called for a water taxi, which deposited us at the Yacht Club. We wanted a drink before we did the customs and immigration thing. One of the great things about the US Virgin Islands is that you don't have to do the *passport* deal—it's part of the United States. How convenient!

I loved the breeze that was blowing, and it was astounding the variations and endless shades of blue and green in the waters there. My words really cannot do it any justice. I felt it was the most gorgeous place I had ever seen, and I had been to Hawaii a few times, but this was more intense of a turquoise color, like my rings.

We exited the taxi and headed for the bar! I ordered a double rum punch; it was frosty, the color of a sunrise and sunset mixed together, and it was *good*. Lorraine had her champagne cocktail, de rigueur. We said our good-byes to the rest of the gang and hung out at the bar for a couple more hours. When we were free at last to move about the island, we wondered if we would be imposing on Cat and Dawn if we asked to crash on either of their floors, or should we get a motel room? When we mentioned it to them, they were incredulous. "Are you kidding? We have plenty of rooms! Please stay with us. We'd hate for you to rent a room." We headed on over. Lorraine knew them well, but it was my first time meeting them. They seemed like sisters! They even *looked alike*: tall, long blond hair, one with big green eyes and one with blue eyes. They were both beautiful. Cat had two children from another marriage; they were towheads like her (never understood that term; I guess it means blond children). Dawn was The Cat Lady; it seemed like she must have had nine or ten! I told Lorraine I would prefer the children to the cats. But Lorraine was also a crazy-for-cats lady, so we flipped a coin. The Cat House, it was.

From the outside, Dawn's house looked great. It was a pale blue with purple trim and a purple front door. It fit in perfectly with all the other bright and pastel houses in the area. In the tropics, the crazy colors just seem normal. There was a riot of bushes and palms and yellow- and magenta-colored bougainvillea trailing across her roof. Very colorful! From where her house sat, you could only see a peek of the ocean from her patio. Just as Lorraine, she had been a former model, but her career was cut short by an unplanned pregnancy, and she decided to become a mom. I did not see her child and did not ask what the situation was (basically, I really didn't want to know).

When we went inside, she apologized for the *mess*, and man, she was not kidding! There was shit everywhere, and I mean literally—the cats were out of control, and she seemed oblivious to the stench and obviously did not do any tidying up! What was it with these beautiful girls that were models and being slobs? Didn't they learn *anything* from their moms?

I went into the kitchen and asked if it was OK if I grabbed a glass of wine, which I did, and made a hasty retreat to the patio for some fresh air. God, it was terrible. Pretty soon they joined me, and she said, "Why don't you guys relax out here? I'll bring out another bottle of wine and some cheese and bread, and it will give me a chance to clean up." I noticed that the kitchen looked fairly clean; it must have been because she, like Lorraine, did almost *no cooking.* Catya was the cook. I made a plan to sleep out on the patio, and as a gesture of thanks for letting us spend the night, I would cook a meal for us all.

I spied five bicycles thrown under the patio and got some money from Lorraine and said I would be right back. "I'm going into town to get some stuff to cook up for dinner." It was only a couple of miles to Red Hook, and I knew the exercise would do me good. It was *great* to be back on land.

I decided to make conch chowder with shrimp for dinner.

Here is how I made the conch chowder with shrimp.

At the fish market, I purchased fresh conch, shrimp, and some crab meat.

You need a *big* pot, and you will cook the conch in the shell for 30 minutes in salted water.

This will be about 15 large shells. When the meat is removed and cooled, you will need a tenderizing hammer or a regular hammer, and you must whack it until it starts to become soft. You will then finely chop it. This would be very similar to what you would do for abalone. It would be inedible if it wasn't tenderized.

Set aside the conch meat on a platter.

Add some butter and some olive oil to the skillet, and chop 2 yellow onions, and fry 4 slices of bacon. Fry bacon until crispy and remove, cool, and crumble. Set on the platter with the conch meat. Stir 2 tablespoons of flour into a glass of white wine and mix well. Add to the pot and stir around to make a thick roux. Make sure you have no lumps.

Add a bottle of white wine. Add 3 cups of chicken broth. Mix this well, and it will start to thicken. Pour in 2 cups of cream. Add a cup of corn that has been sheared off the cob, with a good knife.

Add finely chopped potatoes, tomatoes, diced green pepper, and diced celery. Add 1/2 cup of ketchup, 1 tablespoon of red pepper flakes, 2 bay leaves, 1 tablespoon of Old Bay Seasoning, 2 tablespoon of lime juice, and salt and pepper to taste. Now add all your conch meat and the bacon *and* 1 pound of shrimp without the tails. Stir well, add another pat of butter to the top, and cover with a lid and simmer until the shrimp are bright pink and the conch is tender. Serve with oyster crackers or bread and butter, and pour a good white wine. This is *better* the next day or the next day after that!

Here is what I did with the crab meat I bought.

If you love a good Bloody Mary, then you will flip over this!

Here is a cocktail that I invented.
It is called a bloody crab.

You drink it from a straw, but you also have a long-handled cocktail fork stuck in the drink.

Prepare your Bloody Mary as you always do—cracked ice, Bloody Mary mix, vodka, Worcestershire, lemon, lime juice, horseradish, Tabasco, cracked pepper, celery salt or seed—and shake this well in a container and pour into a tall glass. Garnish with the basic stalk of celery, *but here is the new part*: *add a large clump of crab meat to the top*, insert your fork down into the drink, and add a toothpick with a cherry tomato and an olive. Sip your drink *and* eat your crab all at the same time!

I sometimes add another small dollop or creamed horseradish to the side of the crab meat, and sprinkle it with a tiny bit of paprika. Voilà! *The bloody crab.*

We ate out on the patio and watched a grand tropical sunset and talked about the past, many stories about the man in common with *all* of them (Jean Paul)—some were funny, some tragic—drank quite a few bottles of wine, and when it was fully dusk, I wobbled over to a long bench that had multiple pillows and sat down but then lay down with a pillow under my head, and before I knew it, I had a thick quilt thrown over me. *Ah*, life was good!

I awoke to the croaking of a rooster a few doors down, and the sky was on fire with red-and-purple streaks and the hint of warm orange and peach at the horizon. I had a terrible kink in my neck, and one half of my head was throbbing. First hangover in months! I snuck quietly into the kitchen and made some coffee *and* a Bloody Mary. Hair of the dog, you know I had another one before having coffee, and it totally set me straight. The other ladies would not be getting up for a while, so I took a walk. The roads were dirt; when it rained, it got all mucky. Some of the houses were built up on stilts and were what you would call boonie shacks, but that was Island Style.

They were kept well painted and clean, with lots of blooming flowers, and there would be dogs and chickens around the house, along with all the kids toys. There was a rustic smell to it all, kind of like exotic flowers and mold mixed together—funky and very primeval and tropical. The people were extraordinarily nice and genuine and friendly. When a person saw you, their first inclination was to *smile*. It just made you smile back automatically. I figured I would let Lorraine make all the arrangements for our flight back to Miami, and I didn't want to be involved with all that; it was her thing. I found a few spots where there were tons of flowers, so I began picking some to make a big bouquet to split between our hostesses when we made our departure. I was gone quite a long time, and by the time I returned, Lorraine and Dawn were up, and sure enough, Lorraine informed me that we would be leaving at one that afternoon. She would be going to her apartment in Los Angeles, and I would be going back to Ridgedale Trail in Laurel. We would be departing from (what I thought was Harry S. Truman Airport on Saint Thomas, but I was informed that it was now called) Cyril E. King Airport. It appears there was a horrific plane crash there in December of '70, where a 707 from the States had crash-landed. The plane hit the runway *hard* and literally bounced up approximately forty feet, came down, bounced *hard* again, and went up another thirty to forty feet, slammed down and skidded sideways, and crashed into the side of the embankment. I know there were fatalities and many injuries. The idea was to *change* the name of the airport as soon as possible so as to wipe the memory from people's minds and not put a dent into the travel industry to the islands. We would be leaving that afternoon from Cyril E. King Airport. We took a taxi the ten miles from where we were staying to the airport.

The plane was not very full, so I got my desired seat of a window *and* the exit door, where you could stretch out your legs, with no seat in front of you. I always thought if there were to be an emergency, it would be a very good idea to be right at one of the exit doors. Considering the recent past incident, my idea seemed like a very good one! The two of us did not sit together.

Maybe we needed a little space, since we had been in close quarters with each other for such a long time. I stretched out and slept for quite a while, and when I awoke, I decided to write some letters, mostly to my sister on Maui and to my brother in Reno. I had some colorful tales to tell of my first major sailing trip and my first job as a galley chef to some major players in the music industry. We had a few hours' layover in Miami, so we headed to—where else?—the bar!

Lo and behold! There were three members of the band Sons of Midnight at the bar proper, all dressed in black, which seemed a little out of place in Miami but was normal for the rock crowd. I did not know any of them personally, but Lorraine did, so we barged in on them. Even if Lorraine did not know any of them, she would just say "Hey, I haven't seen you since that time in New York," and they would gladly play along because she was a stone fox (gorgeous). Her sheer physical presence seemed to open any door she wanted to enter, and she used it to the hilt. I wondered what is life gonna be like for her when she gets older and her beauty fades? There wasn't the plethora of cosmetic surgery clinics then as there is today, with famous faces becoming unrecognizable after botched attempts to slow the hands of time. As it turned out, they would be on the same flight as we were, as they too were headed back to the City of Angels.

I always hated flying into LAX! It was always so freakin' crowded, and the smell of diesel fuel was so thick you could cut it with a knife! It was September, and it was over one hundred degrees with the satanic winds blowing straight off the desert, known as the Santa Ana Winds. It sucked every molecule of moisture from your skin, your eyes, and your nose and made static electricity snap and crackle everything you touched and made your hair stand up on end. "Fuck this! Let's just grab our bags and get on another flight outta here to Frisco!" said a grumpy Lorraine as we stood like cattle with the hundreds of others crowded around the merry-go-round of baggage. I had my poke and jacket since I had them with me on the plane, so technically, we were just waiting for *her* big suitcases. It was three in the afternoon, and I knew the traffic would be horrific, but at least, we did not have to drive. The only saving grace of the Santa Ana condition was that because it was an offshore wind, it would blow all the smog out of the LA Basin, and you could really *see* how bad it was when you looked out to the ocean; there was a yellow-brown curtain hanging over the water on the horizon—just lovely. At least we didn't have to walk far, as we spotted her Lincoln limo waiting for us, live parked. She was dropped off at her place, and Chet was nice enough to take me to Ridgedale. We made plans to get together for dinner in a couple of nights.

I felt so strange being back like the twilight zone. I never felt like that before, coming back something was different. I mostly loved coming back to Southern California. I was born and raised in Long Beach, and my dad was born in Venice Beach—there was nowhere else like it in the world.

It was a trendsetting place, and whatever kids were doing in Los Angeles, it soon spread to the rest of the country. So much freedom! I think I was also slightly depressed at the thought of coming back to cleaning houses, after pushing myself so far out of my comfort zone on the Caribbean trip and accomplishing something so complex. I wanted *more* now but had no immediate alternative. No one was around when I got in, and I seriously contemplated going straight back over to Lorraine's to swim in the pool but thought better of it and knew she would be a bitch, plus we were kind of sick of each other. I took a cold shower, lay down, and took a nap. I drifted off with the idea swirling around in my head of possibly having my own restaurant—I could see the sign Lizzy Borden's Beach House, Steaks and Seafood. It would have to be in Santa Monica.

When I woke up, there was still no one around, kinda nice, and it was cooling off since the sun had set, so I walked down the hill to the country store to chat with all the "creatures" that hung about. I checked the shaggy bulletin board and bought a pack of smokes and an iced tea and trotted back up the hill. Wherever you went, you heard music. People would be practicing new songs or just sitting on the porch, strumming a guitar. There was a real feeling of solidarity and community. We all helped each other and shared. The foundation was somewhat shattered when the Manson murder rampage happened, but with time, the paranoia everyone felt subsided. Thinking about steaks and seafood made me realize how hungry I was and how I was mostly craving *lobster.*

I had a fantastic recipe for lobster, and in 1971, it was pretty cheap. I had an aunt named Sherry who loved this dish, and one of the ingredients was sherry, so it was appropriately named.

Lobster Sherry

Here is how you make it.
You will need 8–10 lobsters *alive* (preferably from Maine)
white flour
cream
butter
shredded Monterey Jack cheese (2–3 cups)
fine quality dry sherry
mushrooms, sliced
1 box Ritz Crackers (crush them, 2–3 cups)
1 *large* glass baking dish rubbed with oil
paprika

* * *

Have a very large pot of water boiling. Add a small handful of salt and a tablespoon of Old Bay Seasoning. The most humane way of killing a lobster is to plunge its head first into boiling water; it will kill it instantly. When the lobsters turn bright red after about 10–12 minutes, remove them and let cool completely. Break apart the lobsters, and remove *all* the meat that is possible, and chop into large chunks. Put in a bowl.

In a large saucepan, melt 1/2 cup of butter and add flour. Stir well and don't get any lumps, and add enough cream to make a thick white sauce. Salt and pepper the mixture. Add 1 cup of sherry.

Stir well and add the sliced mushrooms and the lobster meat.

* * *

Pour your hot lobster mixture into the greased glass casserole dish. Add the shredded cheese. Top with the crushed Ritz Crackers. Sprinkle with paprika.

* * *

Bake in a 350-degree oven until the top is browned and the cheese is bubbly.

This is a dish that would be appropriate for a wedding, anniversary, birthday, Christmas Eve, or New Year's Eve. If you want to go *all out*, serve a first course of oyster stew before the lobster sherry. Add some sprigs of watercress on the side for greenery. This dish is *out of this world*!

As long as I could remember, my life had always been about extremes—heavenly highs and drastic lows. Even before my dad kicked me out at seventeen, our family life was the same. My father made extremely good money as a journeyman plumber, but he belonged to a union, and sometimes he would be on strike because he had to. Sometimes he would be off work for a month or two, and that was devastating! He would have to resort to almost any means possible to put food on the table for *nine* people. I remember being about eight years old and he had been laid off for more than three months and it was Christmastime. We had a tree, and we decorated it with the ornaments that my mom had inherited, but there were *no* gifts, or presents, that year. We didn't even have a holiday dinner. We had turkey potpies with cranberry sauce! So I learned very early on how to make do with what I had or figure out what I had to do to survive until something better came along.

The kids did not get off easy either! The boys had to mow lawns, paint people's scuffed-up address markers on the curbs of their houses, pull weeds, trim bushes, etc., and I had to babysit constantly, even if it was a school night. There was one lady who was a widow, and she had two daughters. She had to work, so she served cocktails at a bar near the racetrack; it was called the Turf Club. The girls I had to babysit were both hyperactive and drove me crazy.

The woman would *never* come home at a decent hour. It was always the same; she would come home with some drunk guy, around 1:00 a.m. They would walk past me on the couch, asleep or pretending to, and I would wait about five minutes and knock on her door. The door would open, just a crack, and a hand would come out, handing me something like fifty dollars! I never complained, and I *never* told my parents how much she was giving me. My parents never seemed to care what time I would finally crawl into bed.

I had only been back from the Caribbean for a few days when I got the call that there was going to be a *huge* folk rock festival in Big Sur, California. It all started out as a means for primarily folk artists to get together and have seminars and conferences as to social conscience, music, philosophy, and ideals, and the first one was held in 1964, on the gorgeous grounds of the Esalen Institute, overhanging the crashing Pacific waves and redwoods and forest running down to the sea. These seminars ran their course and evolved into full-blown concerts, using the *music* to put forth the ideals of the folkies. This festival was set for the fall of '71. *All* the foremost musician/singer/songwriters of the day—Joan, Judy, Richie, Mimi, and some bands and even gospel artists—would be performing for a day. It was going to be touted as the Anti-Woodstock or the Anti-Newport Folk Festival. There would be *no* police, or Hell's Angels, as security and the theme was one of nonviolence and making money was not the object! The running rumor was that there was a book and a film planned from the resulting concert to make back some of the cost. Of course, Lorraine and I would be going! As things progressed, I was informed that I was desired as a chef and that the promoters wanted to *pay* me for my services. Now that was going to be a first, and it would be quite a large crowd, approximately three thousand people, including artists and crews and spectators, but it could be more. I would be renting a truck and six helpers, and there would be a large white tent. My lamenting about wanting bigger and better challenges landed right in my lap. After lots of conference calls and research, I came to realize this atmosphere would not be one of outrageousness but of organic wholesomeness, and a large proportion of the crowd were into living off the land and their gardens, etc. I found out from the promoters that a mostly organic, vegetarian menu would be very desirable. I asked about fish, and that was acceptable too. I would have an outdoor cooking venue set up with power. The food would be *free*, but any beverages would be paid for. There were going to be a few other food vendors besides mine, so all the pressure wasn't resting on my shoulders. I would be setting up a whole day before the event and could prepare much of the food the night before.

We decided to leave days early and make the fantastic coastal drive from Los Angeles to Big Sur. I had my rental truck packed with all the essentials and a couple of my girls. Lorraine had her Lincoln, and she had the rest of the crew. As we came through the tunnel and popped out in Malibu and that incredible beach, we knew we were on our way

We had two rooms booked in Pismo Beach, the weather was perfect, and we had a great little restaurant a few steps from the motel. We headed north, after checkout time and would be making our way to the River Inn in Big Sur late that afternoon. We made our way over to check out the venue and located our tent. We were road-weary, but the adrenaline was flowing, and we started to assemble our setup. I made sure we would have lights and power for our prep.

I had everything for the three menu items, except the fifteen *large* salmon that would be delivered.

The salmon was to be grilled on two six foot BBQs, end to end. I would have a little table in between the BBQs to pass out paper plates, napkins, forks, and ladle on the sauce.

I decided to pull an all-nighter, and a couple of my girlfriends volunteered to hang with me.

Here are the recipes.

Pasta Foo Foo Fazoo

penne pasta
whole canned tomatoes
tomato paste

giant cannellini white beans
kidney beans
pinto beans
yellow onions
bulbs of garlic
fresh basil
fresh oregano
fennel
tomato sauce
corn
blocks of white cheese
olive oil
fresh rosemary
salt and pepper

* * *

I had to cook the pasta in three industrial-size pots. The sauce would be in two industrial-size pots. Everything went into the sauce but the cheese. The pasta was drained and added and mixed together with paddles. I had brought approximately fifty restaurant-style heavy aluminum baking pans. The pasta and sauce mixture went into the baking sheets (5 inches deep) and the shredded cheese went on top. They were all covered with tight foil and pierced with a few holes. Ready to be baked until bubbly.

Slammin' Salmon

fresh Pacific salmon fillets
salt and sugar for brining
pepper
real maple syrup
brown sugar
pecans
olive oil

* * *

Coat the fillets on both sides with olive oil, then rub with *lots* of salt and sugar mixed together to coat them well! Let them sit for at least forty minutes. Wipe them off, and recoat with olive oil. Prep the grill (must be clean and oiled well). Salt and pepper the fillets well. Lay handfuls of rosemary branches on top of the coals. Put on grill grates, and BBQ the fish till browned. Prep the sauce. Mix maple syrup with brown sugar and chopped pecans; heat until melded. Spoon sauce over the barbecued salmon!

Naked Al Fresco Fruit Salad

apples
cucumbers
pineapples
white and red seedless grapes
fresh cilantro
lime juice and lemon juice
sugar
flaked coconut
white crème de menthe

Chop your fruits into chunks. Don't peel them; just seed them and core. Do peel the outer part of the pineapple. Roughly chop a lot of fresh cilantro; mix together well. Liberally sprinkle with lime juice, lemon juice, and quite a bit of sugar. Mix well again, and top with flaked coconut, and drizzle portions with crème de menthe.

Just a note: Adjust all these ingredients to the size crowd that you are cooking for.

I mostly made educated guesstimates from my past experience. Just make sure you do things in the right sequence and taste, taste, taste as you are going along, and everything will be fine. Have *all* your ingredients assembled before you begin; have a checklist, and that way, you will be prepared when you start cooking.

The day got under way. There was a thick blanket of fog in the morning, and we were all freezing. Someone had the presence of mind to provide us with steaming coffee! What a godsend! The fog started to lift, and we could hear sound checks starting from the mikes.

We were so busy we didn't pay much attention, but all the press were arriving; the talent, the promoters, interviews were under way, *and* the people started streaming in.

There were super tall poles with brilliantly colored flags and banners, snapping in the wind, and the crowd was just as colorful. The introductions began, and I started fretting about my salmon! Sure enough, a large white delivery truck pulled around the outside and over to our tent. I was *ecstatic* when I saw that the fish was as perfect as perfect could be.

They had done all the work for me, and the giant, fat fillets were gorgeous.

I went behind the tent for a quick smoke break, and there, walking past me, was the *most* excruciatingly handsome man I had ever set my eyes upon. He looked at me, I looked at him, dumbfounded, and a shock ran through my head that I must look a total *fright*!

I hadn't slept at all; my long hair was on top of my head in a big *bun*, my apron was all grubbed out, and I had *no* makeup or whatsoever—I looked like *shit*.

But I could not take my eyes off him. He must have been searching for a head, and I was hoping he would stroll back by. I grabbed my poke, found a mirror, flipped down my hair, brushed it, put on some lipstick, put on a clean apron, and donned some shades well; it was something anyway. There he was, as I had hoped. He was not wearing California-style clothes. He looked like he must be British. He had shoulder-length wavy brown hair, which glinted in the sun with reddish highlights, and his mustache was mostly red.

I had downed a few shots of vodka to bolster my courage and realized if I didn't make a move, we would probably never speak or see each other again. I motioned to him to come over, and he responded. I said, "You aren't from California, are you?"

And he said, "No, I'm from over the pond. My name is Colin, and I'm in the band Tanglewood, and we're fourth on the bill today. I'm one of the guitar players."

I said, "Hey, nice to meet you. I'm Liz, and I'm one of the chefs cooking here today."

He said, "That's brilliant."

I said, "Really?"

He said, "That's absolutely brilliant!"

Well, we hit it off straightaway. I noticed he had dreamy greenish/hazel eyes and a very soft manner, a quiet, almost shy way of speaking, and I was knocked out by his accent.

He confessed he was a bit nervous about the whole affair, and would I like to smoke a joint with him? I said, "Oh, absolutely. I am a bit nervous too, since I'm cooking for hundreds of people." We just fell in with each other so completely and effortlessly. He was shy, but I was more extroverted, and it was a great combination from the beginning. I told him I would be paying close attention when they hit the stage. Tangylwoode was a band that was gaining popularity in the States and was very big in the United Kingdom, their music being a combination of traditional English tunes with electrified guitars and a folk/rock sound I found very appealing.

He was wearing a forest-green jacket, with a smoke-gray turtleneck, jeans, and boots. I was swooning, and I confess, I had a tingly sensation in my nether regions just talking to him. He said he wanted to meet later.

I said, "You know where I'll be."

About this time, we were ready to put the fish on the hot grill. People started lining up, and we had two tables where we had set out all the pasta foo foo fazoo sheets for people to help themselves. We started grilling the fish. In no time, it was char-broiled, and we had the people form two lines.

I had the table in between the two grills, and I started passing out the plates, utensils, etc., and spooning on the sauce. But I noticed I had to reach over the corners of each grill to hand out the goods. It was *hot*. I mean really hot, but I didn't notice at the time; I was in the thick of it and thinking about *Colin*.

After we dispersed all the food and there was still lots of pasta foo foo and naked salad on the tables, I took a breather. I did not want to miss Colin. I took another smoke break behind the tent and noticed

Lorraine in all her finery and glory, schmoozing with people behind the stage. She looked like a tall pink flamingo, with arms waving flamboyantly—she was in her element.

It became apparent to me that we had *done it.* It was agreed that we would bring as much food as we could, and when it ran out, that was it (since it was *free* after all). I had brought six hundred paper plates, and by the time we were out of food, there were twenty-five left. We had served 575 plates of food!

One of the girls noticed that my armpit areas looked inflamed. I was wearing a halter top, which was sleeveless, with an apron, and upon closer inspection, we realized I had second-degree burns and angry-red blisters in my pits! I had to go to the medic, and they put some salve on the burns.

I didn't get to *see* Colin, but I heard him. I was falling in love. I had given him my number in Laurel Canyon and could only hope that he would follow through.

We got home; I had my check for $1,500 and my burnt armpits, but it was a huge success.

I needed a rest! I was despondent that it was two days and he hadn't called. I decided to not get my hopes up.

I was sleeping in, which I never did, and around 1:00 p.m., one of my communal housemates woke me and said, "There's a guy on the phone. He's a limey. He says he wants to talk to you."

I *bolted* to the phone, not really awake. It was *Colin.* He seemed distraught that his bandmates were supposed to leave from Big Sur to San Francisco to fly to some other gig, but he begged off.

He wanted to see me! He was willing to fly to Los Angeles. I told him it was a lovely idea and I really would *love* for him to come. I *begged* Lorraine for the use of her Lincoln and for the driver Chet and I to pick him up. I couldn't believe it was happening so fast. I tried to make myself as appealing as possible and got the house at Ridgedale ready. Candles, music, incense—the whole nine yards. I wanted to cook dinner for him. I asked him what his favorite thing was.

He said, "Your American hamburgers are brilliant! I really fancy them."

"*What? Hamburgers?* Well, OK, hamburgers it is. With *all* the trimmings."

We sat in the back of the car, and before we knew it, we were locked together. Insane kissing, laughing, kissing, laughing. *Then* a little drinking of champagne, provided by Lorraine. I explained as the limo pulled up to our little road that there were many of the best and the brightest of our current music stars, living right here in this little area of Laurel. He seemed impressed. He couldn't get over the fact that there was this place that seemed like it was in the woods but only a short drive down to Sunset and all the clubs. I didn't want to share him with the club scene; I wanted him all to myself.

We drank more champagne, listened to music, and I made him hamburgers.

Colin's Hamburgers

sourdough bread
Parmesan cheese
ground sirloin
dill pickles
tomato
lettuce
thousand island dressing
provolone cheese
apple pie filling from the can
butter

* * *

Melt some butter in a skillet.

Brown ground sirloin patties well. Set aside.

Prep sourdough bread with butter and pat with Parmesan cheese on the outside.

Put burgers back into the skillet, and add the slices of cheese until melted.

Put the burgers with the melted cheese onto the sourdough bread and put into skillet.

Brown the bread.

Turn over and repeat with more butter and Parmesan cheese.

Take off the heat, open up, and add the lettuce, pickle, tomato, and thousand island dressing. *Now add a couple tablespoons of apple pie filling. Trust me on this.*

Secure each side of the burger with toothpicks, and cut in half with a serrated knife. *Burger heaven.*

Don't hesitate with the apple filling. Once you have tried it, you will never forget it. Sounds *crazy* but *works*!

We ended up spending the night together in perfect, harmonious bliss. I have mentioned before that I was nearly six feet tall. Out of the shower, well, Colin was about six feet three inches. We fit together like the proper pieces of a puzzle that just snap together. Perfection.

CHAPTER FIVE

The rest is history. We fell in love. It seemed *so* dramatic to me that he wanted me. I was thrilled but surprised that it all just naturally fell into place. Our relationship was easy. He was such a mellow fellow. But you could see a certain little sadness behind his eyes. It wasn't until much later that I realized that he had a very hard upbringing, for different reasons than why *my* childhood had been so rough, and I was out on the street at such a tender age.

His dad had been a mine worker and died at an early age from lung stones, leaving Colin, his mum, and a younger brother to fend for themselves. Colin was only twelve, and his mother had to take two jobs to make ends meet. Much later, he told me the most vivid thing he remembered of his childhood was always being so cold. His uncle gave him a guitar when he was thirteen, and he threw himself into it. He incessantly borrowed and listened to his mates' vinyl records from the States and taught himself very quickly how to play chords and copy melodies, his relatives saying that he was a quick study. We became so close so quickly. He loved to talk, and we had marathon sessions, which cemented our friendship, as well as our lovemaking. We could not get enough of each other!

I guess he felt sorry for me that Ridgedale was such a dump, and he didn't especially like the communal aspect of it. He and his band were on a roll and taking advantage of the current climate of the popularity of the English folk rock sound, so they were willing to tour and book gigs as much as humanly possible. Straightaway, he wanted me with him, and he had enough money so that I could come along. I could not believe my *good fortune*!

There was somewhat of a sea change going down, and I could feel it in my bones. I was so tired of the uncertainty of how I had been living for the past three years, even though I went on these incredible and amazing trips! It all came back down to those ultra highs and black-hole lows.

Colin was offering me a new life, and I was ready to grab hold and fly away with him. What a coincidence that at just this same time, Lorraine and her on-and-off relationship with Jean Paul was firing up and they were seen around town being all lovey-dovey, not doing their usual arguments in public, and being *openly* affectionate with each other. Maybe the little boy they had, now that he was more of a child than a baby, had something to do with it. He looked like a clone of his dad. She told me she was now ready to rent that cottage on Saint Thomas and she would be moving away and letting her apartment go in Los Angeles. Both our lives were taking 180-degree turns at exactly the same time. It always seemed like we were joined at the hip, but the times, they were a-changin'.

I left Ridgedale as Tangylwoode made its way from the West Coast to the East. The band didn't want girlfriends and wives staying with the bandmates, so there would be a room for me so that he and I could be together as much as possible and so there would be no friction. I made *no* demands on him, so he could still spend as much off time with them as he wished. He thought I was the *coolest* for being an unconventional female. He soon realized I was still a tomboy and wasn't a girly girl at all. I gave him as much freedom as he wanted, and that really worked in my favor!

It made him love me all the more.

When the band had finished up their last date in Upstate New York, he said that he wanted me to come back home with him. I told him he didn't even need to ask! He did not warm up to California or, most especially, Los Angeles. He still very much wanted to live in the United Kingdom and wasn't about to give it up, but lots of the bands eventually did because the taxes in England were outrageous compared to the United States. But Colin and his band were not rich enough to own castles the way some of the English rock and roll royalty bands were. His parents were from a place called Blackpool. That is where he was born and raised. It was a strange place and had sort of a small Coney Island–type of amusement spot that was active during the short summers, where people would come and buy tickets for the rides, test their skills at the games, hang on the beach, and swim and have their fish and chips. It was similar to Liverpool, in that it was mostly hard-working, hard-drinking lower-middle-class people. It was a gray and gritty and pretty grim spot.

We did not go to Blackpool. We went to London, where his uncle Niall lived (the one who gave Colin his first guitar). His wife's name was Miriam. They were his only family left. They lived in a modest, upper middle-class home, with a fenced yard and a little Pekinese dog named Bee-Gee. Niall had been successful at selling real estate in his second career of being semiretired. He *gave* Colin a piece of property with a cottage! The property and cottage were located in an area called Shoreham-by-Sea in the South Downs area of the county Sussex. The English Channel / Strait of Dover were the waterways, and the property was not too far from a city proper called Brighton, Hove, and Worthing.

His aunt and uncle were so formal it was kind of awkward for me, but I could find a way to fit in with anyone, if they gave me the chance. His uncle was wearing a herringbone jacket and dress shirt, and his aunt was wearing a very conservative tweed skirt, well below the knee, and a sweater and scarf with a single strand of pearls. Her hair was pulled back and pinned in a French twist. They were *very* nice and cordial! They were understated but had a wry and very dry sense of humor that seemed to be bounced off one another, like they had been together a very long time. I could tell they liked me and thought that Colin and I were a good match. I wore a black turtleneck sweater, jeans, and boots and a metallic silver trench coat. I had my waist-length hair pulled into a ponytail. As we were having tea, Niall regaled us with stories, and it was obvious they adored Colin, as they never had children of their own.

Niall still spoke of his brother and how he knew he would die very young from working in the mines. He also said that when Colin was about thirteen (about the time he gave him his first guitar), he began to *grow.* No one in the families ever became very tall, so it was incredibly mysterious that Colin reached the staggering height of six feet three inches! I too was amazed by his physique—square jaw, long neck, very broad shoulders, slender waist, and no ass at all—just long, long legs. Maybe a very distant great-great-grandfather? Who could say?

We were invited to stay for dinner, and out of the blue, I asked, "Would it be all right if I cook dinner for us all?"

Colin popped in and said, "She is a brilliant cook, and she would love to do this for us all."

They readily agreed, and Colin and I left to go shopping. I would make them my mom's most requested dish: her pork chops.

Here is the recipe for poor man's pork chops.

(We could afford to buy *thick*, actually *double thick* pork chops, not the sad flat ones my mom used to be forced to buy.)

pork chops
butter
olive oil
thinly sliced potatoes
thinly sliced yellow onion
salt and pepper
Worcestershire sauce
fresh thyme
sauerkraut (drained of all liquid)
fresh parsley for garnish

* * *

In a very large skillet, melt some butter and some olive oil.

Swirl together over medium to high heat. When very hot and a drop of water really sizzles, add your pork chops after you have dried them with paper towels. Do not turn them, just let them really brown.

Flip them, and cook the same on the second side. Remove them and put on a plate covered with foil.

Add a bit more butter and oil. Add your potatoes and onions and salt and pepper and a good bunch of thyme. Cook till they are slightly browned, readd your chops, and nestle them into the potatoes and onions, and completely cover everything with the sauerkraut to the top of the pan. Salt and pepper, and really douse it all with Worcestershire sauce. *Cover* and cook for about 30–40 minutes on medium for all the flavors to blend.

When serving, put *everything* on a *large* platter, and serve family style and sprinkle with chopped fresh parsley for color.

You could serve this with a Rosé wine or a spicy white. Have crusty rolls on a platter with butter for sopping up juices.

Niall insisted on doing dessert for us all, which surprised me! He made poached pears with Devonshire cream with little cookies on the side, and we all had a taste of sherry.

They seemed like they wanted to stay up and talk some more, but I was dusted (a California term, meaning *very* tired). We retired to a very cute little upstairs bedroom, and we both just went straight to sleep. It was a *very* successful evening all the way around.

We begged off having a big breakfast, just tea and lemon cookies, since we were going to make the drive to view Colin's property. When I laid my eyes upon it, I was dumbstruck.

It was somewhat windswept, lush and green, with an ocean view, lots of cottage roses around the cottage. You could tell it was really old but lovely. It was *funny* how low the doorways were, which would take some getting used to for us. I spent a lot of time nursing my head from whacking into the top; it was worse for Colin, but he didn't seem to mind, since he loved the place so much. There were five acres of land.

There was a couple who maintained the property. You could tell it had been recently painted. There was a very big hearth/fireplace, three bedrooms and a bath, with a retrofitted bath in the garage that had been added. There were also what you would call quarters out there, beside the bathroom/shower. There was a couch that folded out into a bed, and a desk—sort of like a bedroom office. There were some animals grazing, and I was informed this was to keep the grass from getting out of hand. I fell in love with this place. It seemed that Colin had known about it for a long time, and he loved it too, but he had no one to share it with *until now.* We hiked a little ways out, away from the house, so I could take some photos, and it was then that he grabbed ahold of me and stared deeply into my eyes and said, "I have dreamed my whole life of meeting someone like you, and now that I have found you, I cannot bear to let you go. Will you spend your life with me and be my wife?"

I didn't even hesitate. I wrapped my arms around his neck and hiked my legs up around his body and kissed him madly, saying "*Yes, yes, yes, yes!*"

We got back to his aunt and uncle's, but they were not there. Even Bee-Gee was gone.

We went up to our room. He presented me with the most exquisite emerald ring. Then he played me the song he had written for me, called "Save Every Day," a lilting, lovely traditional English melody. We were so in love.

A lifetime has gone by. I gave up ever living in the United States again. I was happy as a clam to be wherever Colin wanted to be. We ended up having three children—two boys, only a year apart, then seven years went by, and we had a daughter. Colin's band eventually broke into parts, some of the people moving on to other bands, but the core stayed together.

To this day Tangylwoode still plays dates around England, Colin and the two other friends who originally formed the group, so they were able to retain the name and the rights to the songs. Our sons, Ian and Nels, are in bands of their own, both playing guitar, and they are both earning a living, so they are doing well. Our daughter, Willa, took after me and went to cooking school and is now a chef in, of all places, the Bronx! She's not far off from having her own place, I am sure.

She is a master of nouvelle French/Vietnamese cuisine. We love it when she comes and cooks for us! I did not abandon my passion completely. I have a large greenhouse that Colin built for me so that I can grow *all* kinds of herbs, which I sell to the pubs and restaurants in Brighton, Hove, and Worthington and right here where we live. In the spring and summer, I have a very large cottage garden, where I produce all kinds of vegetables, which I sell, and I conduct cooking classes in the late summer, using all our bounty. I am currently spending this windy and cold winter writing a cookbook. My days of never knowing whether things would be looking *up* or *down* just went straight *up* and never came down, once I met Colin that day in Big Sur so very long ago.

A COOK

They had a cook with them who stood alone
For boiling a chicken and the marrow bones
Sharp flavoring powders and spices to savor
He could distinguish London Ale just by the flavor
And he could roast and broil and sear and fry
Make good thick soup and bake a tasty pie
People revered him so much it would make them cry

—Chaucer
(Traditional poetry in the year AD 1340)

THE RECIPES

1. Chili rellenos
2. Chicken tamales
3. Truffled eggs
4. Fiery eggplant bruschetta
5. Liver Pat-tay mermaid's tail
6. Screaming Yellow Zonkers ala Liz
7. Raspberry turnovers with melted chocolate sauce
8. Dutch lunch steak tartare
9. Keith's shepherd pie
10. Red grouper with potatoes and peppers
11. Corn bread with cheese and chilis
12. Conch chowder with shrimp
13. Bloody crab—vodka cocktail
14. Lobster sherry
15. Pasta foo foo fazoo
16. Slammin' salmon
17. Naked al fresco fruit salad
18. Colin's hamburgers
19. Poor man's pork chops

www.ingramcontent.com/pod-product-compliance
Ingram Content Group UK Ltd.
Pitfield, Milton Keynes, MK11 3LW, UK
UKHW041929190726
13854UKWH00004B/1526